MISCHA

EYE CANDY INK BOOK 2

SHAW HART

BLURB

Love, romance, dating. Mischa Jennings wants no part of it.

He's seen up close and personal how love can ruin your life and he's vowed to stay far away from that emotion. Armed with a set of rules to keep him safe, he's been going through life just fine. Then Indie Hearst comes bouncing into Eye Candy Ink and turns his whole world upside down.

Suddenly, he's breaking every one of his rules, but it's okay. He's not even close to falling for Indie.

Right?

For everyone who read and fell in love with Atlas.
Here's Mischa.
I hope by the end, you're a sucker for him too.

1

Mischa

I SHAKE my head as I watch Atlas practically skip up to the front door. His girl, Darcy, is finally coming in tonight to let him tattoo her and he's been unable to focus or talk about anything else all week. It would probably be annoying if I didn't love the guy so much.

Atlas is a softie. The kind who wears his heart on his sleeve, who always sees the best in people. I can tell that he's already head over heels for this girl and I'm not sure how I feel about that.

I've been looking after Atlas since he came to town and started at Eye Candy Ink. He's like the little brother I never had and I've felt protective of him since he first set foot in the shop. I kept an eye on him at home and in the shop, making sure that no one was messing with him, and everything was going great until my client, Indie, came in with her best friend, Darcy the other week.

Atlas took one look at her and was a goner. Now he's turned into a sap, chasing after Darcy like a little puppy dog. I'm not even sure that Darcy cares about him or sees him like that. Which would make sense. Love is for suckers after all and someone always comes out the loser. One person always gets left behind or loved less. Why most of the population seems so eager to experience the emotion is beyond me.

Atlas and I might look alike but we're polar opposites in terms of personalities. I prefer to keep things light, to have people laughing and joking with each other but Atlas is more serious and introverted. He's also desperate for attention and love, probably because of what his parents put him through during his childhood. My parents put me through some shit during my childhood too, but whereas Atlas craves love and intimacy, I can't stand it.

The rest of the shop doesn't have my aversion to love and most don't share my concerns about Atlas being so far gone already. Zeke, the owner of Eye Candy Ink, says that I'm going to die alone but he's never had a girlfriend or anything close to a girlfriend in the entire time that I've worked for him, so what does he know. Sam is like a little sister, one who doesn't want the details of my sex life and Nico rarely speaks but he does roll his eyes every time I sneer at love and relationships or bring up my rules. I doubt he'd be interested in any details about my romantic or sexual life either.

I follow Atlas up to the front door but he gets stopped by his phone ringing.

"I'll see you at home, Atty," I tell him as I head past him and start to push open the front door.

"See you, Mischa," he says distractedly, and I can hear the smile in his voice.

I push out, heading into the night only to be stopped short when I see Darcy and Indie heading my way. They're both dressed similarly in yoga pants and flip flops. Indie's indigo eyes brighten when she spots me and she grins at me, practically skipping up to where I've stopped on the sidewalk. My heart trips in my chest and I rub the spot. *What the hell was that?* That's never happened before, and I frown. Maybe I should go see a doctor about that.

"Hey, you two! Indie, nice to see you again. Darcy, Atlas has been dying to see you."

Darcy's cheeks flame and I bite back a grin when I see Indie elbow her in the side, shooting her an, "I told you so look". Darcy rolls her eyes in response and she's saved from having to say anything when Atlas joins us outside.

"That's enough," Atlas says, giving me a hard look, begging me not to mess this up for him. I sigh as they awkwardly go through the hello process.

"Hey."

"Hey," Atlas says with a grin, hovering over Darcy.

No wonder he scared her off the first time they met.

"Mischa!" Indie says, scaring me out of my thoughts, drawing everyone's attention to me and stopping me before I can make my escape. "I am starving. You wanna grab a pretzel with me?" She asks, hooking a thumb over her shoulder and pointing to a street cart that looks like it's about to close up.

She gives me a pointed look and I know that she's trying to give the two lovebirds some time alone together. Part of me just wants to head home. Spending more time with the beautiful tornado that is Indie can only lead to bad things but I also know that if I turn her down, she'll go by herself and I can't have her wandering around at night all alone. If something happened to her, I'd never be able to forgive myself.

"Perfect. I was just about to grab a bite to eat," I lie as I force a grin at Atlas, clapping him on his shoulder as I lead Indie away from Eye Candy Ink and over to the soft pretzel cart.

Normally, I don't eat dinner with a girl, or take girls out on dates. It's against my rules, but I calm myself down by reminding myself that this isn't really dinner, more of a snack, and this sure as fuck isn't a date.

I reach for my wallet, ready to pay for my pretzel but Indie beats me to it. She orders four soft pretzels and some water, leaving the change as a tip. She thanks the vendor, beaming at him before she breaks off a chunk of pretzel and pops it in her mouth. She passes me a pretzel and a bottle of water and then tries to juggle the other three pretzels and her own water bottle.

"My treat. I did invite you after all."

"Thanks. I can take my other one now too," I tell her, holding my hand out for another pretzel.

"Your other one?" She asks, confusion on her face and my mouth drops open as she takes another large bite of her pretzel.

I watch in amazement as she finishes off her first pretzel in record time and tosses the napkin into a nearby trash can. I wonder where she puts it all as my eyes assess her. She's wearing a pair of black leggings with a loose tie dye tank top but I know that she's thin.

Indie is tiny and she looks like a pixie with her small curves and dainty features. She's got a Snow White vibe going on with her pale skin and her jet black hair and she'd be easy to overlook until you see her eyes.

They're this fascinating violet, indigo, amethyst color that I've never seen before in real life. I'd never admit it to anyone, because they'd blow it way out of proportion, but I used to have dreams about those eyes. I've lost track of the times that I've stayed up late sketching them, trying to get the color and shape and expression in them just right. I have an embarrassing large stack of papers in my room, all filled with failed attempts to capture Indie to paper. I can never seem to get that playful mischief that's always dancing in her eyes just right.

We walk aimlessly down the sidewalk, enjoying the warm summer night. She finishes her second pretzel and looks at me from the side of her eye before she sighs and splits the last pretzel in half, handing it to me.

"Thanks," I say, grinning at how upset she looks to be sharing her food with me.

We walk down the street together, turning left and heading toward the river as we finish our food. I've never had dinner with a girl before. *This isn't dinner. We're just hanging out, trying to give our friends some alone time.*

"How's your tattoo?" I ask after we've finished eating and have tossed our napkins into the trash.

"Good! I love it," she says, showing me her forearm where the tattoo I did the other week is on full display.

We stop under a streetlamp and I study the tattoo in the dim light, grinning when I see that it's healing well. It's a computer with thorny, blood red roses curling around the keyboard and some type of code written on the screen. I looked up what it meant after she left. It says "And in the end, all I learned was how to be strong alone."

That seems to fit Indie to a T. I haven't spent that much time with her but I don't need to be Nico level observant to see that she's a cool girl. Independent, crazy smart, loyal, and completely, utterly, self-sufficient. She's a tiny little badass... who apparently has the energy of a puppy and the coordination of a drunken sailor.

I grab her arm, jerking her back onto the sidewalk. She was trying to balance on the edge and failed to see the bicyclist speeding her way.

"Thanks!" She says like it was no big deal and like she didn't almost just get run over.

She skips ahead of me and I wonder if maybe Indie is also a little crazy. I grin when she spins around a light pole and jog to catch up to her.

We start walking again, looking out over the dark waves at the water below us. Indie starts telling me about a new app that she's working on and that reminds me of something.

"Hey, do you think you could come check out our scheduling software? I'm sure Zeke could pay you or whatever."

"Sure, what's going on with it?"

"It keeps deleting appointments. It's been happening for a couple of weeks and I swear to God, Sam is about to lose her freaking mind."

"Yeah, I bet! It's got to be hard to do her job if she doesn't know who's coming. I'll have to check my schedule, but I can call you and we can figure out a day for me to come in."

She pulls her cell phone from her back pocket and looks up at me expectantly.

"You can just call the shop. They would know more about that," I hedge. Giving out my phone number is against another rule of mine.

Indie arches a brow at me, planting her hand on her hip.

"Mischa, are we friends?"

"What?" I ask, trying to figure out where she's going with all of this.

"Are we friends?"

"Uh, sure," I say, not wanting to piss off Darcy's best friend. I have a feeling that I'll be seeing both of these girls a lot in the future.

"Right, well, then what's your number. Because friends have each other's phone numbers."

"I-"

"You're making this weird, Jennings."

Hearing her call me by my last name snaps me out of it. Sam calls me by my last name all of the time when we're joking around and she's a girl. *Indie will be just like Sam.* That's what I tell myself anyway as I rattle my number off to her. My phone buzzes in my pocket with a new text a minute later and Indie rolls her eyes at me before she starts to walk again.

"How long have you been at Eye Candy Ink?" She asks once I've fallen into step beside her.

"A couple of years now. I moved here right after I turned eighteen and got hired like right after that."

"Where are you from originally?"

My whole body locks up at the question. I hate talking about my past but I try not to let it show.

"Out west," I say casually, "What about you?"

"I was born in Colorado, but my dad was in the army so we moved around for a few years. He died when I was seven and my mom moved us up here."

"I'm sorry. Is it just the two of you then?"

"No, she remarried when I was twelve and she has four kids with my stepdad."

"Ah, so you're the cool older sister then?"

"Not really. I don't see them all that often."

I can tell that the fact that she doesn't see her family that much makes her sad and I hurry to change the subject.

"When did you meet Darcy?"

She beams at the mention of her friend's name and I can't stop a similar smile from tugging at the edges of my lips. This girl's happiness is contagious, I swear.

"Right after we moved to Pittsburgh. I walked into third grade and sat down next to her. She was this really quiet, shy girl, and I was, well, me," she says with a chuckle. "We've been inseparable ever since."

We turn away from the water, heading back toward downtown and I laugh as she tells me about some of the trouble her and Darcy got up to when they were younger.

"I swear, I remember turning the hose off but when we walked outside the next morning, the water was still running and the front flower bed was a lake. I felt terrible. Darcy and her grandma were always really serious about plants and they worked all summer on that flower bed and I managed to ruin it in a couple of hours."

I laugh, picturing a scrawny Indie standing ankle deep in muddy water and floating plants.

"Were they pissed?"

She gives me a curious look but shakes her head no. *Ah, Indie had the type of childhood where you could make mistakes without getting hit for them.*

"I was a kid and they knew it was an accident. Her grandma was the best. We actually all laughed about it."

We turn back onto main street and head back toward the glowing neon pink Eye Candy Ink sign. I'm glad that Atlas is doing Darcy's tattoo after hours. If anyone from the shop saw me hanging out with Indie, they might get the wrong idea. I've already been dodging questions because they think that I let her hug me after I tattooed her the other week. I've been trying to tell them that she snuck it in but they don't believe me. They'd never stop bugging me if they knew that I went out to dinner and took a stroll with her. *It wasn't dinner and this isn't a date*, I remind myself.

They all know that touching and dates break my rules. When I was a kid, I came up with a list to keep myself safe and ensure that I never fell in love. As long as I follow those ten rules, then my life will remain perfect. Deviate in any way and things start to go off the rails.

Atlas thinks my rules are ridiculous but what does he know? He's chasing after Darcy, blind to the rest of the world. I don't know how anyone else in the shop feels about them. It's not that the other guys are anti relationship. I'm pretty sure that's just me, and *maybe* Sam. Zeke says he's just always been too busy to date or settle down and Nico, well, he doesn't really say much of anything.

We get back to the shop and I dig my keys out, unlocking the front door and leading Indie inside. The door bangs shut behind us but beside that, the place is quiet except for our laughter as we head back to Atlas's room.

"Hey, you two!" Indie says as she bounces into the room ahead of me. I try not to stare at her ass. That isn't a thing that friends are supposed to do after all.

"Hey," Atlas says, his eyes staying locked on Darcy. I roll my eyes at him but, of course, he doesn't notice and Indie doesn't seem to mind his lack of attention.

"Are you all done, Darcy? Can I see it?" She asks, moving closer and trying to peek down the collar of Darcy's shirt.

"I'll show you at home," Darcy says, shaking Indie off of her with a smile. Indie pouts but shrugs, turning back to Atlas. I start to grin at her enthusiasm and hurry to cover it with my hand. It's obvious those two are close.

"You ready to go?" She asks her, looking between Atlas and Darcy.

"Yeah, I just need to pay,"

"It's on me," Atlas says, waving off Darcy's money.

"You don't have to do that."

Dude wants you. He's not going to let you pay.

"I want to. Trust me, it's fine."

"Thanks," she says quietly.

"Anything for you, Darcy," Atlas says and I try my best to hold back my gag but he still sees me and gives me a death glare.

Indie looks back and forth between Atlas and Darcy with a knowing look on her face as the silence in the room stretches.

"See you later, Atlas!" She calls as she turns to me where I'm still leaning against the doorframe. She heads toward me and I straighten from the doorway as she gets closer.

"Thanks for getting dinner with me," she says, raising her hand.

I expect her to high five me or something but she moves quick, raising up on her tip toes and wrapping her arms around me in a hug before she smacks a loud kiss on my cheek and pushes past me and out into the hallway.

Silence follows her actions and I can feel my cheeks start to heat as I try to shake off the shock. *How did I let that happen again?* Normally, my guard is up around people and I've become a master at avoiding human contact, yet somehow, Indie has managed to get a kiss and now *two* hugs in on me. *I'll just have to be more vigilant around her*, I tell myself as Atlas and Darcy finish up.

"Here's the aftercare instructions," Atlas says, handing Darcy a piece of paper.

I step out into the hallway, trying to give them some privacy. They finish talking a minute later and Atlas joins me in the hallway as we watch them leave.

"Ready to go home?" I ask when the door closes behind them.

"Yeah, just give me a minute to clean up."

I nod at him as he heads back into his room and I head into mine. I pull my cell phone out of my pocket, intending to scroll through Instagram while I wait for him to finish up, but then I see the message.

UNKNOWN: PUT ME IN AS YOUR BFF <3

I CAN'T STOP my grin at that request and I bring up a new contact on my phone, saving her number into my phone under Trouble.

2

I ndie

I LOVE MY JOB.

Some people might call me a workaholic but I learned from a young age that you needed to work hard in life if you wanted to succeed and be self-sufficient. I don't need a therapist to know that seeing my mom jump from one guy to the next after my dad passed, always beholden to them for financial support, had an effect on me. She's stuck with my stepdad now who treats her more like a servant and babysitter than his wife. When they got married when I was a teenager, I promised myself that I would never need to rely on a man or anyone else to get what I wanted.

I've probably taken that to an extreme since I work from nine to five at my job and then go home and work on apps until I pass out most nights. It's gotten worse since Darcy and Atlas started dating. With her gone, there's no one to pull me out of work and force me to relax. I make a mental note to take some more downtime for myself as I drive down the road toward Eye Candy Ink.

I've always loved messing around with computers and working at Allied Software is a dream come true. I get to design software for a living and I make a killing. They even let me work from home sometimes and I can design apps on the side without them trying to claim that it's their property too. They also let me leave early, like today, so that I can run errands, or in this case, fix the scheduling software at Eye Candy Ink.

I had called Sam the day after Darcy got her tattoo and we arranged a time for me to come in on Friday. I'd be lying if I didn't pick that day just because I knew that Mischa would be in the shop and I was dying to see him again.

I've thought about texting him the last few days but I get the feeling that Mischa spooks easily. I'm going to have to approach him like he's a wild animal; cautiously and slowly. I know that he likes me too, or at least I think he does. He had seemed interested when we grabbed those soft pretzels the other night.

I've never been that interested in the opposite sex. I've been out on dates before but never had an actual serious boyfriend. I think part of that was because I watched my mom date one loser after another when I was younger and seeing that kind of turned me off to the idea of dating and marriage. Even my stepdad, Kevin, is a bit of a loser. He expects my mom to take care of the kids and house, to have a beer waiting and dinner on the table for him at 5:30 like this is the fifties or something.

He and I don't get along, which is part of the reason why I never go home and see them. Last time I went for dinner, he told me that I was never going to find someone because of my job. He said guys would be intimidated by it because I make more money than them. I had said that I didn't want to date a dumb loser who couldn't comprehend what I did or handle how awesome I was. I didn't need or want a guy whose dick got smaller just because my bank account was bigger or got all weird because of the fact that I could take care of myself. I made it quite obvious that he fell into that second category. He had ordered me to leave and my mom had backed him up. I haven't been invited back since.

That still stings. Shouldn't a mother protect or at least have her daughters back?

Luckily, I have Darcy. Darcy who has been floating on cloud nine since Atlas tattooed her. She came home the next night from their date with her lips swollen and stretched into the biggest smile that I have ever seen. Seeing that only proves that there are good guys out there. Darcy never said it out loud, but I know that she thought that no one would want her because she's curvier than some girls. Atlas is changing all of that. He can't take his eyes off her and I'm so happy that she's finally found a guy worthy of her.

I think it's seeing her so happy that finally has me interested in dating. Now that she has a boyfriend, and one who is sweet and charming, I want to find my guy and I'm pretty sure that Mischa is it. There's something about him that just intrigues me. Maybe it's the way he changes from light and teasing to serious and skittish. Maybe it's that he seems like a challenge and I love challenges. I can just tell that he's hiding something and I need to find out what that is.

My mind drifts back to our pseudo date the other night. He had let me pay and been totally fine with it, not making a big deal out of something that was nothing. He had seemed interested in my job and the app I was making and he hadn't tried to act like he knew more than me about computers or tried to mansplain anything to me. He's basically a unicorn. *MY* unicorn.

I park down the street from Eye Candy Ink and walk up to the front door, smiling when I see Sam and her fire engine red hair through the front window. She looks relieved to see me and shoots me a smile before she turns and yells something down the hallway. I open the door and step into the lobby, smiling at some of the customers waiting to be called back to get tattooed.

"Hey, Sam," I say as I wait for her to get up and unlock the gate that separates the lobby from the back.

"I've got it," Mischa says as he heads down the hallway toward me.

I grin at him, trying not to bounce on my toes as he approaches. He's wearing black skinny jeans that are ripped at the knees and a black Eye Candy Ink shirt. The only speck of color is the logo on his shirt, the bright neon pink standing out against the black. He was wearing all black the other night too and the first time that I met him. *I wonder if he hates color*, I think as I stare down at my leopard print converse, purple leggings and pastel blue shirt with little kittens and yarn all over it. I look back up at him taking in his lean frame. His tattoos cover every inch of available skin from his ankles up to his chin and I lick my lips. I've been dying to see them all since the first time that I met him.

"Hey, how's it going?" I ask once he's closer.

"Pretty good. Here to fix the computer?"

"No, I'm getting another tattoo. I heard Atlas was the best here and-" I cut off abruptly when I see the scowl take over his face. "Jeez! I was just kidding. Yeah, I'm here for the computer."

Mischa nods, rolling his eyes as I follow him through the gate and into the little front office area. I go to set my bag down and my toes catch the edge of a box filled with Eye Candy Ink shirts. I brace myself for the fall, but Mischa catches me, grabbing my upper arms and pulling me upright.

"Careful," he murmurs, glaring at the box before he pushes it out of the way.

"Thanks," I tell him before I turn to see Sam smirking at Mischa.

He crosses his arms over his chest, looking anywhere but at me and I roll my eyes. *Right. Baby steps, here.*

"Thanks so much for coming to look at this. It's been driving me crazy for weeks now."

I smile at Sam, grinning when I see the look on her face. She's glaring at the computer screen with fury and hate glowing in her eyes.

"No problem. I'll see what I can do," I say as I squeeze past her and sit down behind the counter.

"Okay, now, have you tried turning it off and back on?" I ask and I turn to see Sam looking at me like she wants to murder me. Mischa is grinning at me over her shoulder and I smile back before I rush to explain to Sam.

"Sorry, that was just a little IT humor."

"Sorry," she says running a hand through her bright red hair. "This mess has me on edge I guess."

"Okay, give me just a few minutes to take a look and see what the problem is," I say as I swivel back toward the computer screen.

The front door opens and a hot guy that I'd guess is in his late thirties walks in. Mischa straightens and I know instantly that this is Zeke. Darcy has told me a little about the owner of Eye Candy Ink. She was right. He does look like a Viking.

I smile at him and he returns it, his smile growing when he sees Mischa standing behind me.

"I gotta get back to work," Mischa mumbles, turning on his heel and marching back to his room.

I watch him go until he disappears before I turn back to the computer screen and do my best to not think about what his abrupt exit means and focus on the screen and code in front of me. Computers always make sense. You never have to guess what they're feeling or why they do a certain thing. Everything is there before you in black and white.

It doesn't take me long to see where the problem is with the software and I explain to Sam and Zeke that the whole program is corrupted and that's why it keeps erasing everything. I had brought some software that I've been working on and I offer to install it for them. It takes me another hour to get it up and running for them and I spend the whole time acutely aware of the looks they keep giving each other. I know that they both are curious about what's going on between Mischa and I, but the truth is, nothing is. Not yet, anyways.

"All set!" I say cheerfully and Sam sighs as she sits down and starts messing with the software right away. "It should be easy enough to figure out but you can call me if you have any questions," I tell her and she spins around to face me.

"Thank you so much. I swear I almost threw the computer a couple of times this week. I was getting so frustrated."

"No problem," I say with a smile, noticing a guy waiting to check in behind the desk, take a couple of steps back.

Zeke is still leaning against the back wall, his eyes appearing to be assessing me.

"I'll walk you back to Mischa's room," he says as he stands up.

"Oh, I wasn't going to-" but he's already walking past me.

I wonder how he knew that I wanted to see Mischa again. *Was I being obvious?* We stop a few steps away from his room and I shift on my feet, gripping the strap of my bag tighter.

"He's a good guy," Zeke says and I nod.

"I know."

He studies me for a moment before he nods and knocks on Mischa's door.

"Yeah?"

"Computer is fixed," Zeke tells him and Mischa's eyes flick to me.

"Cool."

Silence fills the air between us and the awkwardness is like torture. I look between Zeke and Mischa, wondering what the heck is happening.

"Isn't it your break?" Zeke asks

"Uh, yeah."

"Maybe you want to take Indie here out then. I'm sure she's hungry too."

I realize that Zeke is trying to hook us up. I smile softly at the idea of this big tattooed guy playing matchmaker, but my smile falls when Mischa answers.

"I'm just going to work here. I need to finish a design for a client tonight."

Zeke glares at Mischa, tilting his head toward me as I shift, staring down at the scuffed toe on my leopard print shoes.

"It's alright. I'm going to head out. See you guys."

I spin, intending to make a hasty exit but Atlas's door opens and he spots me.

"Hey, Indie! How's it going?" He asks with a smile. His phone is in his hands and I can see he's messaging Darcy. *Oh my god, these two are so cute.* I smile at him and he starts to walk me up to the front door.

"How's Darcy doing? She's not working too hard, is she?" Atlas asks as he holds the gate open for me.

"No, she's good. You guys going out again?" I ask.

"Yeah, just as soon as I have another day off."

He gets this wistful, dreamy look in his eyes and I grin before I wave and head out the door to my car. I don't look back. I know that Mischa won't be watching me leave. Guess I made up his interest in my head. I try not to let that get me down as I make the drive back to my apartment.

3

M ischa

"You're an idiot," Zeke says as soon as Indie is gone. "Why didn't you take her out to dinner?"

"You know the rules."

"You went out to dinner with her the other night," he points out and I shoot daggers at Atlas's door.

"That was different."

"How?" He asks sarcastically and something that looks like worry passes over his face. He runs his hands through his hair and I shift in my chair, anxiety clawing at my throat.

"I just didn't feel like it tonight," I lie.

Zeke shakes his head, frowning.

"That girls something special and you're fucking it up. I just don't get why. I know you like her. Hell, the whole shop knows that you like her. Why are you pushing her away?"

"You know I don't do love or relationships. Indie is the

relationship type. Besides, I don't want to sleep with her and mess stuff up between Atlas and Darcy."

Zeke looks like he wants to argue but Sam calls his name and he turns to leave. He looks disappointed though and my stomach cramps. I hate letting Zeke down. I hate letting anyone down but I know that I would only hurt Indie in the long run, so isn't it better to stop things before they start?

I turn back to my desk, picking up my pencil and working on my next client's tattoo but I can't push the way Indie looked when she left from my head.

Jesus, she's under my skin already and I've only known her for a few weeks. We've only talked three times! How am I this far gone already? I lean back in my chair, looking across the hall and into Atlas's room. He's seated at his desk, his phone in his hand and I watch as he grins at the screen, no doubt texting Darcy. I'm not sure that I've ever been that happy. But do you really have to be in love or dating to feel like that? I frown, forcing back thoughts of love and dating and most importantly, of one Indie Fucking Hearst.

It's been ten days since Darcy dumped Atlas. I'd probably still be entertaining thoughts of Indie and I together if her best friend hadn't completely smashed my best friend's heart. I can't believe that I had actually been considering breaking my rules and asking her out on a date. Luckily, I was reminded exactly why I had such a hard stance on love and relationships before I did something stupid, like take her out to dinner.

Atlas has been moping around all day, all week actually. He keeps staring glumly off into space or checking his phone every five seconds and it's driving me crazy. I've tried to cheer him up, to distract him, to talk to him about it but nothing has worked. He doesn't want me and admittedly, I'm probably not the best person to talk about broken hearts or relationships with but I'm trying. He doesn't want me though. All he wants is Darcy.

My phone beeps and I spin around toward my desk, swiping it off the counter and checking to see who could be texting me.

TROUBLE: Is Atlas as miserable as Darcy is right now?

MISCHA: IDK, is Darcy staring at her phone like it holds the meaning to life and listening to the same sad song on repeat?

TROUBLE: No, if anything she seems to be avoiding her phone. I hate seeing her like this.

MISCHA: Well then maybe she shouldn't have broken up with Atlas and crushed his fucking heart.

TROUBLE: Maybe he shouldn't have been kissing other girls.

MISCHA: He didn't kiss anyone. The guy is so far gone on your friend that he doesn't even notice other girls.

THERE'S a pause then and I grip my phone tighter.

TROUBLE: We need to fix this.

MISCHA: Tell Darcy that Atlas isn't the type to cheat.

TROUBLE: I'm not sure she'd believe that coming from me. Let's just lock them in a room together until they get past this.

MISCHA: I think that might be a crime.

TROUBLE: Yeah, but I know that you're still in.

She sends me a gif of bad boys and I bite back a grin, trying to figure out how to get Atlas and Darcy to talk to each other. I know that if they just sat down and listened to what really happened that they would be able to work through this and then they'd be back together in a heartbeat.

MISCHA: Think you can get Darcy to Captain's Bar tonight?
    TROUBLE: Maybe.
    MISCHA: We'll meet you there. 9 pm.
    TROUBLE: See you then.

My heart kicks in my chest at her response and I rub the spot absently as I bite my lip and shove my phone into my pocket as I head back towards Zeke's office.

"Hey, I'm going to take off a little early. I don't think we'll get any walk-ins tonight and my last client just left."

"Where you headed?" He asks and I know he's surprised. I'm usually the last one to leave this place.

"Just out," I hedge.

"To see Indie?"

"No, Darcy," I blurt out without thinking.

Zeke's eyebrows rise, blending in with his shaggy blond hair.

"Why would you go see Darcy?"

"Just trying to talk some sense into her. Atlas would never cheat on her or anyone. Maybe if she hears it from someone who knows him, she'll believe me and give him another chance. The dude is miserable."

"Hmm," Zeke hums, leaning back in his office chair.

"What?" I ask, crossing my arms over my chest.

"Just funny how the guy who doesn't believe in love is now the one trying to play cupid."

I can feel my cheeks turning pink and I shift on my feet.

"Try being the one who has to live with him when he's like this," I grumble.

"Uh huh."

"I just hate seeing him sad. He's going to mess up a tattoo and take this place's whole reputation down. Then I'll have to find a new job and-"

Zeke laughs, an easy smile splitting his lips.

"Whatever you say, Mischa."

"So, I can go?"

"Yeah. I'm not going to stand in the way of you and true love."

"Oh my god," I groan as he starts making kissy faces and curving his hands into a heart.

I can hear him laughing the entire time I walk down the hallway to leave.

"What's so funny?" Sam asks as I head out through the gate.

"I don't know. I think Zeke has finally lost it," I grumble as I wave goodbye and jog down the sidewalk to my car.

It's only 6 pm and I know that Darcy works until at least then because Atlas mentioned it about a hundred times in the last two weeks, so I hurry and drive the few blocks over to her nursery. I figure this conversation will go better if Indie isn't there listening to me yell at her friend. I pull into the parking lot and frown when I see all of the lights are off, but then I spot one lone car, parked off to the side and I pull in next to it.

I turn the ignition off and walk quickly across the parking lot to the front door before I can change my mind. The door is locked so I knock, watching as a shadow comes out of the back and walks closer to the door. Darcy sees me and frowns slightly but unlocks the door after I smile and wave at her.

"Hey, Mischa. What are you doing here?" She asks as she shuts and locks the front door behind her.

"We need to talk. About Atlas."

She freezes and doesn't turn around to face me right away. She looks pale but I can't tell if it's because of the low light or if it's her.

"What about Atlas?"

"He's miserable, Darcy," I spit out. *No point in beating around the bush, right?*

She closes her eyes and I can tell that she really is as miserable as Atlas. My heart softens in my chest and I sigh.

"I know that you haven't known him that long but you have to know him better than this. He would never cheat on you. He's the best guy - the most loyal guy - that I've ever met."

"I saw him with-"

"You saw some girl hit on him. It happens to him all of the time. Girls throw themselves at everyone in the shop pretty much daily but we never take them up on it. Atlas has never been like that. He's not the one-night stand type of guy. Dude, I'm not even a hundred percent sure that Atlas has ever even had sex!"

Her mouth drops open and I realize that maybe I shouldn't have said that last part but I push on.

"Listen, Atlas might look like a tough guy but he's actually pretty soft. He... he's never really had a lot of people who care about him. His parents work constantly. He never really talks about them but I know that they were never there for him when he was growing up and they still barely talk. He told me he only had one girlfriend in high school and from what he said, it sounds like he was only with her to make his parents happy. She cheated on him and they broke up and he didn't even seem to care."

I stare at her hard, waiting for her to figure out what that means but she seems blank. I sigh again, my fingers tightening into fists.

"Do you even get what that means? He was with that girl for over a year and he didn't care when they broke up. He was with you for a couple of weeks and he's fucking devastated. All Atlas wants is to be loved. He's honestly a little desperate for it and I thought maybe he was rushing things with you, but... he dated that girl for a year and .... What do I know? Maybe love really can happen that fast. Maybe you really do see someone and just know."

"I-I..."

"Just listen to me right now, okay? Atlas is starved for attention, for someone to love. He hates being on his own. I mean, we both make enough that we could have our own places but he still chooses to live with me. And I don't mean that he just chose you randomly and that's why he likes you. I mean that he finally found someone that clicked with him. There's something about you that just fits with him. I thought you were going to be good for him but you just ended up breaking his heart," my eyes narrow on her after I say that and she looks away.

"Atlas might come on a little strong, but he means well. I just wish that you would have let him explain. I wish that you would give him a chance."

I spin around, more than ready to get the fuck out of here and forget that this ever happened but I realize that I can't just leave her here in the dark.

"I might be upset with you for hurting him but Atlas would kill me if I didn't make sure that you made it to your car okay."

We walk in silence the short distance to her car and I wait until she's safely inside before I head over to mine and slip behind the wheel. Now, I just need to head back and grab Atlas and pray to God that Indie can convince Darcy to come to the bar tonight. I can't take much more of seeing heartbroken Atlas.

4

————

I ndie

By some miracle, when Darcy got home tonight, she actually wanted to go out. Relief flooded me that she wasn't going to spend another night on the couch, watching sad movies and eating ice cream. I mean I would do that with her every night for the rest of my life if that's what she needed but I know that she's not happy. She needs Atlas and from what Mischa said, he needs her too.

I pull into the parking lot at Captain's Bar and check the time. 9:15 pm. We're a little late but I have a feeling that Mischa and Atlas will still be here.

"I'm glad you came out with me. I know the last couple of days have been rough so let's go in there and relax. Try to have some fun, yeah?"

"Yeah," Darcy says, her voice lacking any trace of excitement but she leans over the center console and hugs me before we both slide out of the car and head for the front door of the bar. I send up a silent prayer that this plan works out and things go well as Darcy and I head inside.

It's crowded inside and we have to push and squeeze our way through the crowd to the bar. I wave down a bartender and order us each a cocktail as my eyes scan the crowd, searching for Mischa and Atlas. I'm just about to text him and ask if they're still here when the crowd parts and I spot Atlas at a table in the back.

I turn back to Darcy and see that she's seen him too. Her eyes are locked on Atlas and she's biting her bottom lip as she watches him for a second. I'm about to suggest we go say hi when she surprises me and starts to turn to leave. I hurry to grab her elbow and keep her rooted next to me.

We watch together as Mischa walks over and sets a beer down in front of him as he takes the chair across from Atlas. Atlas barely looks up but I catch a glimpse and can see the dark circles under his eyes.

"He looks miserable," I say as we continue to stare across the bar.

The bartender places our drinks down in front of us, giving me a flirty look but I just slide a twenty across to him. Darcy picks up her drink, downing half of it in one gulp and I follow suit. *Apparently, we're going to need liquor tonight.*

"Maybe you should go over there and talk to him," I suggest as I take another, smaller, sip of my drink. Darcy opens her mouth to protest but I cut her off.

"Just hear me out. You've been miserable ever since you two broke up and look at him. He's clearly in hell. I know that he's still texting you and trying to talk to you and you have to know that he really does like you. I know that you were upset about seeing him and that girl but, Darcy, he was just doing his job. Guys don't keep texting and calling if they aren't seriously into the girl."

I point over to their table and then suck in a breath when I see that two girls have joined them at the table. I watch as Mischa shoots a nervous look toward Atlas. For his part, Atlas doesn't even seem to realize that there are other people at the table, or in the room. He hasn't looked up from his phone since we've gotten here.

One girl reaches out to touch Atlas and he jerks back at the contact, shooting the girl a dirty look as he sits back further in his chair. I watch his lips, trying to catch what he says to her but it's too dark in here to make it out. Whatever he says has the girls taking off quickly and I smile as they head to another table. *Thank god.*

Darcy and I lean against the bar and finish our drinks slowly as we continue to watch their table. Three other girls try to come up and get close to him and he turns them away quickly each time. I smile more every time he turns them away and after the last one, I turn to Darcy.

"If he didn't want you then he could have taken any of those girls up on their offer. He doesn't know you're here so it's not like he's turning down sex for your benefit."

She looks back to him and we both watch as he starts typing on his phone. Darcy's cell buzzes a second later and I grin. *She's found the perfect guy. Meanwhile, I'm over here chasing after one who can't seem to get away from me fast enough.* I push those thoughts aside and turn to her.

"He's out and he's still texting you, Darcy. That guy freaking loves you and I know that you really like him too. You let your mom leaving you mess with your head but it wasn't your fault. She left because she was weak, not because of anything that you did. She should have chosen you, she should have been a better parent, but the drugs clouded her vision. You let those kids in high school put things in your head but they're not true. They weren't back then and they aren't true now. You've always been gorgeous and I think that you were finally starting to see that with Atlas. You were happier, more confident with him. He's good for you and you're good for him. You need to start seeing yourself more clearly and you need to trust Atlas."

We set our empty glasses on the bar top and I hug her.

"Trust *ME*, Darcy. That guy is never going to do anything to hurt you. Give him a chance."

She hugs me back tightly and all is right in the world.

"Mischa came to see me after work tonight.," she whispers against my shoulder and my whole body goes stiff.

Why? What could he have possibly said to her? Is that why she wanted to go out tonight?

"What did he want? Was he bothering you? Is that why you wanted to come out tonight?" I ask all of the questions that just ran through my head.

"He just wanted me to give Atlas another chance."

We're silent for a moment and I look back to where Mischa is seated. He's wearing all black, as usual, and it's hard to make him out in the dim light.

"Will you come with me?"

"Of course," I say as I turn and lead her through the crush of bodies and over to their table.

I smile at Mischa as we finally come to a stop in front of them. Atlas looks up with an annoyed look on his face, probably expecting another pair of girls and his eyes widen when he sees Darcy and I standing there instead.

"Darcy," he says as he jumps to his feet.

"Hi, Atlas. Hey, Mischa," Darcy says, waving at both of them.

"Hey, Darcy, Indie," Mischa says with a relieved smile as he stands to greet both of us too.

Atlas hasn't looked away from Darcy once and I smile wondering if he even realizes I'm here as well.

"Hi," Darcy says again.

Ugh, she's so awkward.

"Hi, hey," he sputters.

*Oh my god. He's **just** as awkward.*

"Hey!" I say, breaking the silence as I take the empty seat next to Mischa.

"Can I get you a drink?" Atlas asks.

"No... I was wondering if we could go somewhere and talk?"

He eyes Darcy nervously and I want to laugh.

"Yeah, yeah, of course."

He looks over to Mischa and I stiffen when I feel him rest his hand on the back of my chair. I turn to look at him and he smiles at me.

"I'll get a ride home from Indie," he says, nodding at them.

Darcy looks at me, hopeful and I can't ruin this for her. I give her a thumbs up and wave at both of them as Atlas leads Darcy away. As soon as they're out of sight, I turn to Mischa.

"Funny."

"What is?" He asks, leaning closer to me to hear me over the loud music.

"You didn't seem to want to have anything to do with me the other day, but now you're volunteering me to give you a ride home."

I arch a brow at him as he leans back in his chair, his hand wrapping around the back of his neck as he winces but remains silent.

"It's weird seeing you sit so still."

"Why is that?"

"Besides the fact that the last few times I've seen you, you've been ignoring me or running away?" I say, taking one last dig at him for the other day before I let it go. "I don't know. It's just that you always seem to be moving. Even when you were tattooing me, you were tapping your foot or nodding your head to the music. You have this weird energy about you. Like you're incapable of sitting perfectly still for longer than a few seconds."

"I'm sorry about the other day."

"You've been avoiding me for a while," I mumble and his stormy blue eyes lock on my purple ones.

"I like you, Indie," he admits and it sounds like it kills him. "but I'm just not a relationship guy. I don't do dating and love and all of that nonsense."

"All of that *nonsense*?" I ask incredulously.

"I've seen up close what it can do to people. How it can destroy them and ruin their lives. Love is for suckers and I'm never going to be a sucker."

His eyes are hard and I want to ask him what her name was, who hurt him like this, but I don't think that he would answer me. Mischa has always been so secretive. Never talking about his past or why he doesn't like being touched. I watched him tense up and shrug off those girls' hands tonight and I've watched him when we were together. He doesn't let anyone get close to him, making jokes and constantly moving so that people keep their distance.

I love a good mystery and there's something about Mischa that calls to me. I've never been the one-night stand type or the friends with benefits type, but no one has ever made me feel like Mischa does before.

"Alright."

"Alright?" He asks, watching me warily as his fingers start to pick at the label on his beer bottle.

"Let's just have sex then."

He freezes, his whole body locking up as he watches me. He looks like a deer in the headlights as he sits perfectly still.

"Are you ready to go now or did you want another beer?" I ask after he hasn't said anything back to that.

"I- This feels like a trap," he says as he eyes me suspiciously.

"Hmm. Well, you can sit here by yourself for the rest of the night, or you can come home with me and find out. What's it going to be?"

He studies my face, his eyes probing, looking for some kind of hint but I just grin at him as I climb to my feet. I take one step and he's on his feet too, following silently after me out to the parking lot.

The drive back to my place is quiet and short. I can feel Mischa watching me the whole time and I try not to make any sudden movements. He follows me up to my apartment and waits while I unlock the door. As soon as it closes behind us, he grabs me, spinning me and pressing me against the wall as his lips come down on mine.

He presses me into the hard brick wall and I moan, my fingers tangling in his messy brown locks. His lips are soft but firm as they move against mine and he steps into me. It's like he can't get close enough and I nip his bottom lip, soothing the spot with my tongue.

I can feel Mischa's hands working between us and then the jangle of his belt buckle opening fills the quiet room. I fist my hands in his shirt, tugging him against me as I wrap one leg around his waist. *Thank god I wore a dress tonight.*

Mischa grabs my hips, boosting me up and I instinctively wrap my legs around his waist as my hands go to his shoulders, steadying myself as we continue to eat at each other's mouths. Part of my brain can't believe that this is finally happening and I know I should tell him that I've never done anything like this before but I don't want to pull my mouth away from his. He tastes like beer and mint and I'm drowning in his taste, so much so that I don't notice when he pulls my panties to the side and positions the head of his cock against my opening.

He thrusts into me and I tense, my legs becoming like boa constrictors around his waist as I try to breathe through the pain. Mischa is still as a statue and I tilt my head back, wondering if he's even breathing.

"You're a virgin?" He asks, his brow scrunching together over his dazed eyes. He says it like he doesn't know how that could be possible and I shift on him, both of us moaning as he sinks deeper inside me.

"Well, not anymore...because you just took my virginity. My flower if you will," I say, blinking my eyes at him and I think that he's going to drop me and bolt. I grin at him, rocking forward experimentally and he glares at me before his eyes get hazy again. I like the way I can make him do that and I rock my hips more, bouncing slightly.

"I'm pierced," he says and I try to focus on where we're connected.

"It feels nice. What is it?"

"Jacob's ladder."

"I don't know what that is. You'll have to let me see it later."

He just blinks at me and I wonder how sex usually goes for him.

"Let's do this *thang*," I stress and a startled laugh escapes Mischa.

"Jesus Christ. Stop talking. You're going to ruin the mood."

I grin against his mouth, pushing my tongue past his lips to tangle with his. His hands dig into my ass and he slowly pulls out before thrusting into me just as slowly, letting me get used to his size and the row of piercings that run up the underside of his thick cock.

"I'm not going to break, Mischa. It feels like you're making love to me, not fucking me."

He growls, biting my bottom lip until I gasp. His hips punch up then, pounding me against the rough brick wall. I can feel it pulling and scratching against my dress and I know that I'll have to throw it away after this but holy fuck, will it be worth it. He fucks me against the wall roughly until sweat beads on his forehead. I tilt my head back against the wall, my eyes falling shut as I feel my orgasm brewing. It expands inside me, starting as a tiny spot until it's spread throughout my whole body. I let the waves of pleasure wash over me and I hear Mischa bite back a curse and something that sounds an awful lot like my name as he finds his own peak.

I blink my eyes open, my violet ones meeting his dark blue. We're both flushed and panting as we watch each other like two wary predators. I'm expecting him to run and I think he's expecting me to declare my love for him.

A noise comes from down the hallway and I realize that Atlas and Darcy are here. Mischa pulls out and lets me down to my feet slowly and I feel his come dripping down my inner thigh. As if he just now realized that we didn't use protection, his face fills with horror.

"Shit, Indie. I've never- I've always used a condom. I don't know what I was thinking."

He runs his hands through his hair and I lean against the wall, my legs still shaking slightly from that rough ride.

"I'm on the pill. And I'm clean," I say, putting him out of his misery.

We're both fully dressed and I don't know where we go from here. I don't want him to leave though and I think if he gave me five minutes, I would be ready to go again. Maybe we can try some different positions this time.

"Okay." I say, waving my hand as I try to shakily stand from the wall.

"What?" He asks and I'm pleased to see that he still hasn't seemed to have recovered yet either.

"Let's go see this ladder."

I head down the hallway, grinning when I hear him follow after me.

5

Mischa

OH MY GOD. What the fuck did I do?

I've been staring at Indie as she sleeps in bed next to me for the last few minutes, wondering what the hell I had been thinking last night. Sure, it had been the best sex of my life, but *fuck*. Rule #5: Never get involved with someone you know. I'm going to see Indie all of the time now that Darcy and Atlas are back together. Not to mention I broke Rule #3 too; Never spend the night.

I've got to get out of here.

As quietly as possible, I slip out of bed and silently pull on my jeans. I never did manage to pull off all of my clothes last night. I try not to be happy about that as I grab my shoes and head out to the living room. I look back toward Indie's room one last time before I pull open the front door and head down the stairs to the street.

My stomach churns and my feet feel like lead as I walk down the stairs. I know my rules by heart but I've already broken half of them for Indie and nothing bad has happened. I haven't fallen in love with her and she seems to be on the same page. I turn left and start to head to my apartment as I think about Indie and this thing between us.

Maybe we could do this? We could hook up and just hang out. I mean, I like Indie. She's a cool girl and as long as we're both on the same page about what this is, then where's the harm? Sure, it would be breaking some of my rules, but I won't break the last one. Rule #10: No falling in love. *I'll hang out with Indie while Atlas is all over Darcy. We'll have sex and everyone will be happy. I'll get her out of my system and then we can go back to being friends or just seeing each other when we have to hang out with Darcy and Atlas. Maybe after this I can finally get Indie out of my head because I haven't been able to stop thinking about her since the moment that I saw her.*

I don't know how long I've been stopped on the sidewalk outside the bakery down the street from Indie's place but it must have been a while because the employee behind the counter is giving me a weird look. I know I might look a little scary or like a criminal to some people, with my tattoos and ear gages. I roll my eyes but then head inside. I'll bring Indie some breakfast. *She's going to need the calories after last night*, I think with a smirk.

I order her a muffin and some coffee before I head back to her apartment. This doesn't really count as getting her breakfast. I'm just trying to be nice before I ask her if she wants to keep having sex with me. And yes, I'm aware that asking her that breaks Rule #4; No sleeping with a girl for more than one night. But I mean, I made that rule before I slept with Indie. Last night was explosive. No one could resist another night with her.

I let myself back into her apartment, tip-toeing through the living room and down the hall. When I push her door open, she's sitting up in bed, already awake. Her head turns when I walk in and she beams at me when I hold up the paper bag with her muffin in it.

I try not to think about the way my heart beats faster when she smiles at me like that as I sit on the edge of the bed and pass her the coffee cup and muffin.

"Morning," she says, her voice raspy from sleep.

"Morning. I got you some breakfast."

"I can see that. Thank you. You didn't have to do that."

She pulls the muffin out and unwraps it, taking a big bite.

"Uh, I had fun last night," I say, looking down as I rub the back of my neck.

"Yeah, me too."

She smiles at me around her bite of muffin and I take a deep breath.

"Maybe we could do it again sometime?"

"Mischa, are you asking me to have sex with you again?"

There's a teasing lilt to her voice and I roll my eyes.

"Say it," she sing songs and I can't help but tease her back.

"What do you say we do this *thang* again sometime?"

Indie throws her head back, her bright laughter ringing out in the quiet room and I can't help but laugh with her.

"Yeah, Mischa. I'll call you," she says as she throws her legs over the edge of the bed.

I stand too and shuffle my feet.

"I should head home. I've got to be at work in a couple of hours."

"I'll walk you out."

We get to her front door and I turn to tell her goodbye

once more but she throws herself at me before I can get any words out. Her arms are wrapped around my neck and I stiffen at the contact but then her lips land on mine and I forget all about her breaking Rule #6; No touching outside of sex.

I back her up against the wall where I kissed and took her virginity last night and she slips her tongue in my mouth. I moan when I taste the sugar from the muffin she just ate and her hands tangle in my hair, pulling me closer to her.

I pull away reluctantly, knowing that if we make out for much longer that we'll be headed back to the bedroom and I know that I don't have time for another round with the delectable Indie.

I set her back down on the ground and step back. Her eyes are dark purple and look like they're glowing in the pale morning light. My fingers itch for my pencils and drawing pad.

"I'll text you later," she says and I nod, turning the door-knob and heading out into the hall.

This is going to be good. Everything will be fine, I tell myself as I head back to my apartment. I tell the little voice inside me who says I'm a sucker already to shut the hell up.

6

I ndie

INDIE: You free tonight? (To do this thang)

    MISCHA: Let's never say thang again.

    INDIE: I can't promise that.

    INDIE: We doing this THANG tonight or what?

    MISCHA: Jesus...Yeah, I can come over at 9.

    INDIE: Cool and then I'll be coming.

    INDIE: LOL!

    INDIE: Mischa did you see what I did there?

    INDIE: Mischa?

I GRIN at my phone before I toss it onto the couch cushion next to me. He might act like he doesn't like it but I know that Mischa is just as weird as I am. We've been texting a bit over the last couple of days and he's sent me some of the craziest memes. I bite my lip, grinning about the one with baby Yoda that he sent me last night. I check the clock and see that I have half an hour until he'll be here.

Darcy is headed over to Atlas's place tonight and she just left so Mischa and I will have the whole apartment to ourselves. I look around and see that it's mostly clean so I pull my laptop onto my lap, grabbing my headphones from my backpack and slipping them on. I can get a little more work in before he gets here.

The next thing I know someone is ripping the headphones from my head and I look up into Mischa's scowling face.

"Hiya," I say, hitting save before I close my laptop and set in on the couch cushion next to me.

"You're going to get murdered."

"Is this a sex thing?"

"What? No! You can't leave your door unlocked. Someone else could have walked in here and killed you."

"Well, then I'm lucky that it was just you," I say, bouncing up to my knees on the couch.

I rest my arms on the back and look up at him.

"Lock your door from now on," he says, leveling me with a hard stare.

"Fine, fine. Are we going to do this *thang* now?"

He rolls his eyes, dragging his hand down his face and I grin at how dramatic he's being.

"Say it."

"Absolutely not," he says with a scowl but I can see the corner of his lips tick up.

"Say ittttttttt," I sing, drawing out the it part and I get an outright laugh at that.

My heart flips over at the sound. Mischa seems to spend

most of his time trying to make other people laugh and I love when I can make him do it for a change.

"Let's go do this thang," he mumbles and I jump to my feet on the couch.

"Woohoo! Did you hear that everyone? Mischa Jennings just said that we're- umph!"

I'm cut off by Mischa grabbing my hands and pulling me over his shoulder. He swats my ass as he carries me down the hallway and into my room.

"Crazy," he mutters but he's smiling when he drops me down onto the bed.

"You like my crazy."

"You can't prove that," he says with a straight face and I grab his waist, rolling until he's sprawled out on the bed with me. We almost roll too far and he grins as he grabs my shoulder and keeps me from falling off the side. We grin at each other for a beat and then Mischa seems to come to and realize how intimate this feels. He blinks, leaning forward to whisper in my ear.

"Take your clothes off Indie. Let's do this thang."

He doesn't have to tell me twice. I pull at my clothes, tugging my shirt off and tossing it toward the corner of the room where my hamper is. My bra quickly follows and I wiggle out of my jeans and panties next, noticing that Mischa seems to be distracted by my small jiggling tits. His eyes are locked on them and I grin as I finally free myself from my jeans and toss them over the side.

"Your turn," I say, pulling at his shirt.

His eyes widen and he seems to grow pale. I remember last time we had sex he had kept most of his clothes on, but I just thought that was because we were too frantic to have each other. I mean he took my virginity against the wall in the living room, two steps into my apartment.

My eyes narrow at him, trying to figure out the problem. He's in great shape so his body can't be the reason.

"What's wrong?"

"I don't like taking my shirt off," he mutters and I frown harder.

"Why?"

"I just don't."

"The lights are off. I won't be able to really see anything," I say softly.

"I don't want you to touch me either."

"Cool, cool...Hey, how did you see this going?"

He chuckles but the sound is bitter with a hint of something that sounds an awful lot like self-disgust.

"Is this about the stuff when you were younger?" I ask quietly and I wince when I feel his whole body tense. I can feel him pulling back, pulling away, and I don't know how to fix it.

"Sorry. You don't have to talk about it if you don't want to."

We're silent for a long time, both of us watching out the window as more and more city lights pop on.

"My parents were... they loved each other. Until my mom didn't. We were fine when I was a little kid. I remember us being fine. I remember us being happy," he says with so much conviction that, for a second, I wonder who he's really trying to convince here.

"Then, right before I turned six, my mom left. One day she was there and the next she was gone. I never saw her again," his voice is flat, dead, and I can suddenly see why he hates the notion of love so much.

"My dad was never the same. He loved her so much and then she was just gone. He was sad for a couple of years but then he got mean. He would drink and then smack me around. A couple of times he would hit me with his belt. He said I looked just like her and he couldn't take it. He drank himself to death when I was seventeen and I spent eight months in foster care before I turned eighteen and headed here."

"You didn't want me to see the scars?" I ask softly.

He doesn't answer me but I can feel the bed move as he nods his head yes.

"I'm sorry that happened to you, Mischa. So fucking sorry, but I'd never judge you or think less of you because of them. Chicks think scars are sexy," I say, trying to lighten the mood before we both drown in the sadness. Suddenly, I get why Mischa is always cracking jokes. This dark place we just found ourselves in sucks balls.

Mischa is still silent so I try again, this time saying something that I know will get a reaction.

"Do you want to just like, cuddle, or something?"

"Oh my God," he groans but he rolls over onto his side and takes his shirt off. He drops it off the side of the bed quickly and lays back down before I can see anything. His hands move to his belt buckle next and he makes quick work of undoing his jeans.

He strips quickly and quietly and I can still feel his unease in the air, the memories from his past back and threatening to ruin this for him, for us. As soon as he's naked next to me, I rise and straddle him, kissing his lips once before I trail them down his chest.

"Your nipples are pierced," I tell him as I lick one nipple and then the other.

"Uh huh," he says but his voice comes out husky and hazy.

I want to touch them, to play with the rings and see how it affects him but the story he just told me and him admitting that he doesn't like to be touched are still ringing in my head. I keep my hands firmly planted next to me on the bed and the only source of contact is my lips on his skin, brushing down his abs and happy trail until they bump into the purple head of his cock. There's already a drop of liquid forming on the tip and I swipe it up with my tongue, licking a line up the row of piercings before I open wide and wrap my lips around him.

"Fuck, Indie," he groans as I start to suck up and down his length. I work my mouth up and down his shaft, savoring the salty taste and musky scent of him. I'm not sure how to navigate the piercings running up the underside of his cock so I just run my tongue over them, moaning as I remember how they felt rubbing inside me.

I've never sucked a cock before, let alone one with as much hardware as Mischa's but judging by his sounds, I'm doing just fine. His abs contract with every swipe of my tongue and I grin when he starts to moan louder. His hands are fisted in the sheets next to him and when I look up at him through my lashes, I can see that his attention is focused solely on me and what my mouth is doing to him. I still haven't touched him with my hands but my fingers itch to trace over the lines of tattoos that curl up his thighs and run across his torso.

"Ride me," he orders and I give his cock one last lick before I crawl up his body, straddle him and slowly sink down onto his cock.

His eyes lock with mine and we both stare at each other, mouths open wide, as I take inch after inch of him. I pause when he's fully seated, reveling in the feeling of being stuffed so full. Mischa's hand comes up and we watch together as his inked hands rub up my stomach and cup my small breasts in his palms. I'm so pale, so plain compared to him and I wonder what he sees when he looks at me.

"You're beautiful," he murmurs, like he heard my thoughts.

I want to tell him that he's beautiful too, inside and out, but I have a feeling that will send us back to that weird place that we just escaped from so I don't say anything. Instead, I lift up and sink back down. I ride him at a slow, even, pace, enjoying the way the ridges of his cock and the piercings drag against my nerve endings. He pinches my nipples, not urging me on but seeming unable to lay still either. I smile at that, tipping my head back and moaning when he leans up and sucks one stiff peak into his mouth.

Eventually, my pace picks up, my orgasm building in my bloodstream until I can't hold back any longer and I cry out his name as I shatter.

"Fuck," he moans, his fingers tangling in my ink black hair as my orgasm triggers his own.

I fall forward, rolling to the side at the last second so that we're not touching. We lay in the dark for a minute, catching our breaths and enjoying the highs from our releases.

"How come you never shut your blinds?" He asks out of nowhere.

"Hmm?" I ask, cracking one eyelid open.

"They were open last time I was here too."

"Oh, I don't know," I say, frowning. "I guess I just never think about closing them."

"You know people can probably see in here. When you're changing or... having sex," he says and his voice takes a speculative tone as he says that last line.

I shift next to him, squeezing my legs together as my core clenches and starts to heat once more. I've never told anyone about my public sex fantasies but leave it to Mischa to figure it out.

"Yeah, I guess you're right," I say quickly, and luckily for me, he drops the subject.

"I should get going. I need to be up early to run some errands before work."

I frown at him as he starts to sit up in bed.

"You can spend the night. Take a shower and leave in the morning. We could do this *thang* again," I offer, trying to lighten the mood.

"We really need to stop saying thang," he says with a laugh and I sit up next to him.

"Stay," I plead and he looks away from me, toward the window.

"I can't. I'm sorry."

He pulls his clothes on quickly, leaning over the bed and kissing my forehead.

"I'll lock the door on my way out," he says as he stands and practically bolts from the room. I frown after him but what else can I say? A second later, I hear the front door close and I collapse back into bed.

Okay, recap. Yeah, he didn't stay the night, but he did take all of his clothes off and open up a little bit about his past. Tonight was still a win, I think as I roll over onto my side and close my eyes. I can still smell him on me and my sheets as I drift off to sleep.

7

M ischa

I'D NEVER ADMIT it to anyone but telling Indie a little about the scars and when I was younger actually felt kind of good. I try to tell myself it's just because now she knows why I don't want to be touched and I can enjoy the sex more but I think it might be more than that. It did break Rule #4: No telling people about my past and Rule #8: No meaningful conversations, but at least I was able to follow Rule #3: No spending the night.

It's been a couple of days since I've seen Indie but we've been texting more than ever. No one can make me laugh like that girl. I love the way her mind works and how comfortable she is with herself. *No, not love.* I can't believe I even just thought that.

I shake my head and lean over my desk, finishing up the last part of the tattoo I'm working on. My client will be here any minute and I don't have time to get distracted by thoughts of Indie.

"Mischa! Your client is here," Sam calls and I drop my pencil as I spin around in my chair and go out to greet them.

It's two girls waiting up front and they grin and check me out as I come out to introduce myself. I force a smile to my lips as I hold my hand out to the first one.

"Hey, I'm Mischa."

"I'm Claire and this is my friend, Meghan," the platinum blonde one that I'm tattooing tonight says.

I lead them back to my room and help them get settled before I show Claire the design and we talk about placement one last time. They keep giggling and the sound is high pitched and grating on my nerves. I rub at my forehead, tuning them out as I ready my equipment and fill some capfuls with ink.

"You'll just need to take your shirt and bra off so we can get the outline on," I say as I start to turn around to face them. Before I'm even done saying the words, she's got her clothes off.

I force another smile her way, ignoring the way she keeps thrusting her tits at me as I slip my gloves on and place the outline against her skin. It's running up her ribs, ending right under her left breast. I get it centered right before I pull the paper away and study the lines.

"Like what you see?" Claire asks, her voice husky and I look up to her.

"All that matters is that you like it," I say, grabbing a mirror and showing her the outline to okay.

"I love it," she says but her eyes are on me and not the ink.

"Great, then we can get started."

I grab my needle and fit it to the machine, turning it on

so the buzz drowns out their voices. She jerks as I start and I try to hold back my sigh as she whines and winces through the next two hours. Her friend holds her hand and tells her it's going to look so hot as I make little line by little line.

Finally, it's done and I lean back, examining it.

"That's so hot," her friend says and Claire preens under the praise.

"What do you think, Mischa?" She asks, shifting so her tits bounce as she turns to look at me.

"Looks good," I say, grabbing some ointment and bandages so I can get these two out of here.

"You know, Meghan wanted to meet you too. We've both heard so much about you."

"Uh huh," I say, not looking up from what I'm doing.

"We love doing things together," she says and it takes me a second to realize that she's coming onto me and offering me a threesome.

My mind flashes to Indie and I freeze. I should take these two up on their offer. I'm breaking way too many of my rules with Indie but these two don't do anything for me. Right now, all my dick wants is a clumsy, purple-eyed, crazy girl with hair the color of midnight who uses words like thang.

As if she can sense that I'm thinking about her, my phone dings and I see TROUBLE flash across the screen. My cock hardens behind the zipper of my jeans and I try to bite back my smile as I wheel my chair over to answer her.

TROUBLE: Thang time tonight. 9:15 pm. Be there or be squared!

· · ·

I ROLL my eyes and before I can respond, another message pops up.

TROUBLE: RSVP to Sex God by 8 pm.

JESUS, this girl? I ask my dick and he jerks in my pants, dying to feel her wet heat wrapped around him again.

MISHCA: I'll be there.
    TROUBLE: Thank you so much for RSVPing!
    MISCHA: You're ridiculous.
    TROUBLE: Call me your sex master from now on.
    MISCHA: Absolutely not.
    TROUBLE: We'll see...

I CHUCKLE as I toss my phone back down but the scary part is that she might be right. Indie has already gotten me to break half of my other rules.

"Are we all done?" An annoyed, high pitched voice asks behind me and I realize that my client and her friend are still in the room.

I spin around to see that Claire is still sitting shirtless on the table and I clear my throat.

"Yup, all finished. Let me just get you the aftercare instructions."

The girls huff as Claire pulls her shirt on and they both head for the door. I follow them up to the front and hand them off to Sam before I head back to my room. It's 8:45 and I have just enough time to clean up before I have to leave for

Indie's. I rush through picking up the mess in my room and spin to head out, coming up short when I see Zeke standing in the doorway.

"Hey, man," I say, pushing my desk chair in.

"Have a good night, Mischa," Zeke says with a knowing smile before he turns and heads back to his office.

I frown after him but let it go. I'm starving and I pop into the pizza place down the road before I head over to Indie's apartment. I try to tell myself that this doesn't break Rule #2: No buying a girl dinner or breakfast. I was hungry so I really got the pizza for myself. If Indie wants a slice then I'm just being polite.

I climb up to her floor, heading for her door. I knock and then growl under my breath as I reach for the doorknob and check to see if it's unlocked. I smile when it doesn't move and a second later, I hear the lock unclick and the door swings open to reveal Indie. Her hair is piled on top of her head and she's wearing round glasses that kind of make her look like an owl. *Why does that work for me?* She smiles at me, her teeth flashing as she opens the door wider to let me in.

"Oh, you brought us dinner! Thank God, I'm starving!" She says as she rips the box from my hands and carries it into the kitchen. I should correct her and say I didn't bring her dinner but my eyes snag on her swaying hips and ass and I get distracted. That's what I tell myself anyway.

She sets it down on the counter, grabbing a slice as she grabs two plates from the cabinet. She's already finished one slice and is reaching for a second when I join her in the kitchen.

"Please, help yourself," I say dryly.

"I'm going to need the energy for when I rock your world in a minute," she says before she takes another large bite.

I love how smart she is. She always has some snappy comeback on the tip of her tongue. We eat in the kitchen, both of us leaning on the counter as we devour the pizza in silence. We finish off the whole pie and then Indie leads me over to the couch, collapsing onto the cushions.

"I ate way too much," she complains, rubbing her flat stomach.

I sit down next to her, laying back against the cushions as she grabs the TV remote and starts flipping through the channels.

"What did you want to watch?" She asks as she flips through the channels at about a million miles an hour.

"You. Coming on my cock," I answer her and she grins at me before she tosses the remote to the side and lunges for me. I laugh as I catch her and pull her up into my arms, carrying her down the hallway to her room.

Like I expected, her blinds and curtains are pulled back, showing off the view of the city below. I know that she brushed it off last time but I could tell that the idea of people being able to see her had turned her on. I'm going to test that theory tonight.

I walk past the bed and over to the wall, setting her down next to the glass.

"Strip," I order and she shifts, her eyes flicking to the window.

Her nipples pebble inside of her shirt and I grin.

"Do you need help?" I ask, stepping forward into her space.

She nods, lifting her hands above her head and I reach for the hem, pulling it up and over her head. Her small tits are bare and I lean down, licking each bubblegum pink nipple in turn before I reach for her yoga pants and push them and her panties down her legs. She steps out of them and reaches for my jeans button. I pull my shirt off while she makes quick work of pulling my jeans down.

I back her against the wall, dropping to my knees in front of her and pulling one of her thighs over my shoulder and opening her up for my mouth. I lean in, breathing in her sweet cotton candy scent before I dive in. I lick up her center, circling the tiny nub until she's rocking her hips against my face, riding my mouth. My hands join the fun and I rub my thumb against her clit as I nip the inside of her thigh, pulling back to look up her body at her.

"You like knowing that anyone could look up here and see you getting your pussy licked?"

"Mischa!" She cries out, her body flushed a pretty rose color as her indigo eyes meet mine. "I need you," she says, holding her hand out to me.

"You'd rather they looked up here and saw you getting fucked against the wall?"

I swear she almost comes from my words and I smile against her pussy lips. Her hips rock as I suck her clit into my mouth, worrying the tiny bundle of nerves with my tongue.

"Mischa! Please, I want you inside me."

She's panting, her eyes heavy and filled with lust. I try to burn that look into my memory, determined to draw it and get it just right as soon as I get home.

"You want me to stuff you full of my cock? Do you like the size or the piercings more?"

"Both! Please fuck me," she begs, her hands wrapping in the strands of my hair as she tries to pull me to my feet.

I give her sweet pussy one last lick before I stand and lift her into my arms. She wraps her legs and arms around me and I almost tense up when her hands brush against one of the scars on my back but then her hot cunt brushes against my cock and that's all that I can focus on.

I lower her down onto me, impaling her on my length and she mewls as my piercings drag along her inner walls. I pin her against the wall right next to the window and I start to thrust up into her. She bounces on my cock, her body rubbing against mine as we move together.

"You think anyone can see you taking this big cock?" I growl against her neck and she lets out a sob, her pussy clamping down around my length. "You want me to take you out to a club and fuck you in some dark corner where anyone could walk by? Where anyone could see you coming?"

"Fuck!"

"Your pretty pussy likes that idea," I say. Seeing her so strung out on my cock has it starting to swell inside of her.

"Mischa, I'm- I'm coming," she shouts and a second later I feel her go off.

Her pussy floods my cock and her hand slams against the window as she tries to keep her balance as I fuck her through her orgasm. Seeing her hand against the fogged-up glass sends me over the edge and I come inside her, holding myself still as I fill her up with my come.

Her legs are still wrapped around me and one hand is still curled around the back of my neck as she rests her head back against the wall. She's flushed, her hair a little sweaty and sticking to her forehead but god, she's still so fucking sexy.

Better than any threesome.

I'm startled by that thought and I push it away, pulling us away from the wall and carrying her over to the bed where I lay her down for round two.

8

I ndie

IT'S BEEN three weeks since Mischa and I started sleeping together. Three weeks of bliss, of ever so slowly peeling back his layers and learning about the man behind the mask. Three weeks of falling in love with him.

We have a routine, one that I'm sure is against his rules but that hasn't stopped either of us yet. He stays at my place and we hook up every night that Darcy stays with Atlas. I love Darcy but I'll admit, I've started wishing for the nights when she'll be gone.

Mischa finishes up at Eye Candy Ink around 9 pm most nights and he heads over as soon as he's done. Sometimes he brings pizza or takeout with him and we eat and watch tv for a bit and sometimes he shows up and is on me as soon as the door opens. I can't decide which nights I like best.

I realized I loved him after the first week, after he

opened up to me about his scars that second time we hooked up. I don't know what to do about my feelings now. I've been trying to slow them down, to hide them from him but every day the words seem to be on the tip of my tongue and I'm afraid I'm going to just blurt out that I love him and never see him again.

I know that he made his feelings clear about relationships but he's broken some of his other rules for me before. Can he really not be feeling what I feel? I've been debating all week what to do. I had originally thought that I could just keep things the same but I need more. I want more with Mischa and if he's never going to want a real relationship or a future with me, then I need to get out now. *I guess I'm just not built for friends with benefits.*

I'm startled from my thoughts as the front door closes and I tense. Did Mischa just leave without even saying goodbye? I pad barefoot down the hallway, the towel wrapped around my wet hair starting to come loose with each hurried step.

"Hey!" I say when I walk into the living room and see Mischa standing shirtless by the couch as Darcy gawks at him from her spot over by the kitchen. I head toward her and grab a glass and the orange juice out of the fridge, pretending like everything is normal and Darcy regularly comes home to find Mischa half naked in the living room.

"I'm just headed out. I'll see you guys later," Mischa says as he tugs his shirt on and heads out the door without a backward glance.

I sigh as I watch him go and I can't help the frown that spreads across my face.

"What's going on with you and Mischa?" Darcy asks and I debate what to tell her, stalling for time by drinking half of my orange juice.

"We're friends... and a little bit more."

"And you're... you're okay with that?" Darcy asks and I can hear the surprise in her voice.

"Yeah, it's cool, Darcy. I like him, a lot. He's just got some hang ups about relationships and stuff, but I'm okay."

We're silent for a minute as we both try to believe what I just told her. I wonder if she can tell that I'm in love with him.

"Just... don't let him hurt you, okay? I don't want to have to kick his ass."

I smile at her, taking the two steps and closing the distance between us so that I can wrap her up in a hug. She smiles at me and comes to give me a quick hug. Man, I love this girl. I've missed having her around here.

"So, enough about me. How was last night?" I ask, heading into the living room and plopping down on the couch.

She sits down next to me and tells me about showing up at the shop after hours and surprising Atlas. I oh and ah at all the right spots, squealing with her when she tells me how they both said they love each other. I'm so excited and happy for Darcy. She deserves a great guy and Atlas is perfect for her. I only wish that Mischa and I could have what they have. Darcy bites her lip and I can tell she's nervous to tell me the next part.

"He asked me to move in with him."

"OMG, Darcy! That's great. I'm so happy for you two. You deserve a good guy like Atlas," I say, bouncing on the couch cushion and dragging her into another hug.

"You're not mad that I would be leaving you?"

"No! We'll still see each other all of the time and it's not like you're moving that far away. I'm so happy for you guys."

She hugs me again and we hold each other for a minute before we pull away and cuddle on the couch together.

"I'm going to miss living with you," she whispers and I nod my head against hers.

"Me too, but this is good, Darcy."

"Guess I should start packing," she says after a minute and I giggle next to her.

"I'll help. We can make a party out of it."

I drag Darcy down the hall and we spend the next several hours organizing her stuff and packing up what we can. We'll need to go get boxes for the rest of her stuff but we can do that tomorrow. Darcy thanks me and hugs me goodbye before she heads back to Atlas's for the night and I check the clock. I never texted Mischa and I wonder if he'll just show up here. My question is answered a minute later when there's a knock at the door.

"Hey," I say, opening the door wider for him to come inside.

"Hey, did Darcy tell you the news?"

"Yeah, that's great, huh? That they're taking that next step?"

Mischa's back tenses and I realize that maybe I wasn't being as subtle as I thought.

"Yeah, I'm happy for them," he says, eyeing me like I'm a wild animal and I realize that this is it. This is the moment. I need to tell him how I feel. My throat gets scratchy as I try to keep the tears at bay, because deep down, I know that this is where I lose him.

"I know that you don't- didn't want a relationship, that when we started this, we agreed it would just be sex but that changed for me," I rush out. "I want more with you. I want a real relationship and I know that you hate that word but we are basically already in one."

"Stop," he whispers, looking shell shocked and horrified but I can't.

"We spend most nights together,"

"Stop," he says louder this time.

"I love you, Mischa."

His reaction would be comical if it wasn't breaking my heart. His eyes dart around the room like he's looking for a way to escape but I'm still standing in front of the door.

"I love you, and I want to date you. I want to be your girl-friend, I want us to be exclusive. We're basically already there. We eat food, hang out, talk, and it's been good. It's been good, right? All that would change is the title."

I try to reason with him but it's like a brick wall went up and I feel the first tear slip free as I watch him stand still and emotionless.

That alone feeling that I've had for most of my life pulses inside of me, growing inside of me with each second that passes as I wait for him to say something. It spreads and takes over my whole body, leaving me feeling empty and hollow. I gasp for a breath when I feel the ache form in my chest where my heart used to be. Mischa still hasn't said anything and I can't take the silence any longer.

"Mischa, I need you to say something," I say as I brush away a few stray tears and try to compose myself.

"You agreed to this. You can't just change the rules all of a sudden."

"I'm not changing the rules, Mischa. I'm trying to play a different game."

He scowls at me for a second before he looks away, crossing his arms.

"I want more, Mischa," I try again, lowering my voice. "I know what we agreed to when we started this, but things have changed. I'm allowed to change my mind. My feelings are allowed to change. I'm not trying to trick you or force you into anything. I just want to know what you're feeling too. How do you feel about me? About us?"

Silence greets me and I look up into his stormy blue eyes.

"Mischa?"

"I can't. I can't do this, I can't do more," he whispers and my heart breaks at the hopelessness that I hear in his voice.

I nod my head because deep down, I knew that the last few weeks had all been leading toward this. Mischa has heartbreak written all over him and I knew that and still took the jump. I shouldn't be surprised when he's not there to catch me.

My mind flits back to this morning when we had been laughing in bed together. Why can't he see how good this is between us? Why can't he see that we're not his parents? I love Mischa but I don't want to be with a guy where I have to force him to be with me or give him an ultimatum and with that in mind, I straighten my shoulders and meet his eyes.

"Then I can't do this anymore. I'm sorry, Mischa, you need to leave."

He searches my face, looking for a way to convince me to just continue with what we had been doing and I can tell the moment he sees that I'm serious. His head hangs between his shoulders and he stuffs his hands into his jean pockets.

He walks by me and out the door without another word and I lock it behind him, turning and sliding down the hard wood. I wrap my arms around my knees and sob, the tears wetting the fabric of my jeans as I cry for everything that could have been with Micha and I.

M ischa

I'VE BEEN WATCHING Indie all morning.

We're all here helping Darcy move her stuff in but somehow Indie has been able to ignore and avoid me the whole time. At her place I hadn't really noticed. I mean, she stayed in Darcy's room, finishing up the last of the packing but that had seemed normal. Then we got here and she's somehow avoided being in the same room as me for the last hour and a half. *It's a small two-bedroom apartment. How is that even possible?*

She left with Darcy about twenty minutes ago to go get everyone breakfast, leaving Nico, Sam, Zeke, and I to help Atlas with the last of the boxes.

"Thanks for all the help guys. We really appreciate it."

I want to gag. *Since when did Atlas become a 'we'. This is what relationships do to people. They make you lose your own identity. Suddenly you're not Atlas anymore, your 'we' and then your Mr. and Mrs., and then you're dead.*

I don't say any of this out loud of course.

Nico just nods before he heads out to the living room and Zeke slaps Atlas on the shoulder. "Anytime, man," he says as he trails after Nico, giving me a weird look as he goes. Sam gives Atlas a side hug before she follows them out to the living room to wait on the food, leaving just Atlas and me alone in the bedroom.

Why did she have to say the L word to me? Indie and I were doing great. Why did she have to ruin that?

I've been yo-yoing between hating her for saying it and wondering if maybe she was right and what we had really was a relationship. Maybe I could keep doing that. She can call it whatever she wants and we can just keep what we had. Then I realize that Indie will always want more. If I give in now, she'll have me saying I love you in another month. Then what? Marriage?

"You okay, Misch?" Atlas asks, pulling me from my spinning thoughts.

I watch as he hangs up some of Darcy's clothes and I wonder if I really am okay. Maybe Atlas can help me here.

"How did you know that Darcy was the one for you?" I ask slowly, already knowing that I'm going to get shit for this. I look over at Atlas and it looks like his jaw is about to hit the floor. I tense, waiting for him to start teasing me but it never comes.

"I just knew when I saw her. She's smart and talented but so kind and compassionate and strong too. A lot of the girls we meet at the shop are ... one dimensional? They only seem to care about their looks or their image, you know? How many followers they have and the newest Instagram filter and bullshit like that. None of that interests me. Darcy is different. She just makes me happy. I know it happened fast but even from the beginning, she was the first person I would think about when I woke up and the last thing I would think about before I fell asleep at night. When she wasn't talking to me, it felt like death. Worse than death. I've never cared if any other girl blew me off but I cared with Darcy. Oh, and the sex is out of this world. I mean the-"

"WHOA! Don't need to know that," I almost shout, holding my hands up to stop him from continuing.

He smirks at me and I pretend to gag as he hangs up some more of her clothes.

"She was just different," he continues and I watch him as he smiles. *Jesus, just thinking about her has him grinning like a lunatic. Wait, do I look like that when I think about Indie?*

"I think sometimes you just meet someone and then BAM! There's just chemistry or something and you know that they're the one for you."

I nod when he finishes. Indie and I have chemistry but that's never been our problem. The question isn't, 'Is Indie the one for me?' It's, 'do I want to have a one?' I've spent my whole life being sure that I didn't, that I never wanted to give anyone that much power over me, and then three weeks with Indie Hearst and I'm rethinking my whole life's motto.

"Is this about Indie?" He asks, right as the front door opens and Darcy and Indie call out that the food is here.

"Thank God, I'm starving," I say, dodging the question.

I shoot him a smile that doesn't quite reach my eyes and turn and head towards the kitchen before Atlas can ask me any more questions about Indie. I head out to the living room and spot Indie right away. She's plastered against the front door and I can tell that she's about to go.

"I'll see you guys later! I've got to get to work," she calls as she turns the knob and walks out.

My heart drops as I watch her go and I head into the kitchen grabbing a breakfast burrito from the bag and taking a seat on the couch between Zeke and Nico. I unwrap the burrito, rubbing my chest where it aches and I wonder briefly if I should lay off all of the greasy takeout I've been eating. Must be getting heartburn or something.

"You alright?" Zeke asks as I take a bite of my breakfast burrito.

"Why does everyone keep asking me that?" I ask, exasperated.

"Cause Indie couldn't get away from you fast enough today," Nico says from my left in his usual no nonsense tone. I turn to glare at him. He shrugs, unaffected and I return my attention to my breakfast.

"I don't know what you're talking about. I'm fine."

Out of my periphery I can see Zeke shaking his head and I hear Nico snort on my other side.

Great, what I hate more than relationship talk.

Pity.

10

I ndie

IT'S BEEN two weeks since Mischa and I broke up. I guess I can't really call it a breakup since we were never in a relationship. That doesn't stop it from hurting like one though.

I haven't talked to or seen him since I helped Darcy move in with Atlas. I don't know why, but part of me thought that maybe he would realize that he loved me too and come banging on my door, begging for me to take him back. Guess I've been watching too many romance movies.

The only good thing that's come out of all of this has been my work. I've managed to finish two apps and I'm ahead on all of my projects at work. With Darcy gone, I've spent every night after work at home. I grab a quick bite to eat before I grab my laptop and work on the couch. I pass out there and if I'm being honest, I know it's because I don't want to sleep in my bed. It still smells like Mischa and I can't bring myself to wash the sheets.

Darcy is supposed to come by with tacos tonight and we're going to watch the episode of Barry that we missed last week together. As if my thoughts conjured her, the front door opens and she comes bustling in, her cheeks a rosy pink and a smile stretching her lips. Living with Atlas really seems to suit her. I've never seen her this happy before.

I smile and go to hug her, digging in the takeout bag with my other hand. She laughs and swats me away.

"Grab us some plates, would ya," she says, pulling out some tacos and a burrito from the bag.

I grab two plates and pull out the margarita mix, shaking it at her.

"You restocked!" She says excitedly and I laugh as I grab the blender and the tequila.

She makes up our plates while I make the margaritas, adding salt to the rim on mine. I've already got Barry ready to go and we hurry over to the couch, digging in as I hit play.

We make it through the first fifteen minutes before she attacks.

"You know, Mischa has been asking about you."

I stuff my last taco into my mouth so I won't have to answer her.

"He asked me how you were doing this morning when I brought Atlas some lunch at the shop."

"I'm fine," I lie and I look down at my plate, scraping up a few strands of cheese that managed to escape and popping them in my mouth.

Another taco lands on my plate and I look over to Darcy.

"I know you don't want to talk about him, but I'm here if anything changes," she says softly and I can tell that she's worried about me.

"Love ya, Darcy."

"Love you more," she says right as Barry comes back on.

I eat my new taco, chewing slowly as I try to pay attention to what's happening on screen. *Why would Mischa be asking about me? He was the one who didn't want more.* Barry ends and I flip the channel over to Bob's Burgers, burrowing back against the couch cushions.

We finish our first round of margaritas and I get up and make us another as Darcy tells me about things at the nursery and what's it like to live with a boy. I tell her about a new project coming up at work that I think I might get picked for and soon we're both lying on the couch, our eyes drooping. I smile, thinking this feels just like old times, before my eyes drift shut and I fall asleep.

11

M ischa

I FINISH ORGANIZING my desk and stretch my arms out, trying to shake out some of the tension from my shoulders as I wait for the shop to officially open. I run my hands through my hair, tugging lightly on the ends before I reach for my coffee cup. I drain the last of it, sighing as I lean back in my chair.

I haven't been sleeping well the last few nights and I know I'm relying too heavily on caffeine during the day, but I don't know what else to do.

I keep having nightmares, the same one every night. I'm walking in a desert, the sun beating down on my back. I'm thirsty, so thirsty and I keep falling in the sand. Then I hear a voice and I look up to see Indie standing in the distance next to this oasis. The water shimmers in the light and Indie smiles at me, urging me to come to her. I smile back, getting to my feet and starting to run toward her but she keeps getting farther away. Suddenly, the sky turns dark and it gets harder to see her. Indie calls out to me, begging me to join her, and I run faster, but I can never quite reach her in time and she slips away. Then I'm left all alone in the dark. I always wake up right after that, my heart racing and that, now all too familiar, ache in my chest, and I can never seem to fall asleep again after that.

I should probably talk to someone but what-

"Hey, Mischa!"

I startle in my chair, almost tipping over backwards, but I manage to catch myself and spin around.

"Hey, Zeke," I say, eyeing him warily.

He's been acting weird ever since we helped Darcy move. He keeps watching me and frowning. I think he knows that Indie dumped me. *She didn't dump you, asshole. You were never together, remember? You don't do relationships.* I try to shake the bitter thoughts away, ignoring the way that they've started to sound more and more like my dad's voice.

"What's up?" I ask when he just keeps leaning against my doorway.

"You alright, man?"

I swallow, hating the sympathy I see in his eyes and the way his voice drops, like he's talking to a scared child.

"Yeah, I'm fine," I say, but I can't quite get my voice to sound like my usual upbeat self.

Zeke frowns and I can tell he's about to say something else but Sam calls for him up front.

"Zeke, the cash register is jammed."

He sighs, pointing a finger at me. "We're not done with this conversation."

"Okay, dad," I say with an eye roll. He flips me off, stalking back up front to fix the register.

I spin back in my chair, facing my desk when a throat clears behind me.

"Oh, Jesus Christ," I mumble under my breath, spinning back to face the door.

Nico is standing there, filling up the entire doorway.

"You're being an idiot."

"Thanks, man," I say sarcastically, but he doesn't stop there.

"You were happy with Indie. Happier than any of us have ever seen you and you just threw it away because you were scared. Now, you're miserable."

My mouth drops open. Nico always gets to the point but this is the most that I've ever heard him speak and I'm too surprised at hearing him say so much that it takes me a minute to recover and catch what he's saying.

"Nico, I'm *FINE*," I stress but he shakes his head, stepping into the room and closing my door behind him.

"I like you, Mischa. You're that annoying little brother that I never had. We all want to see you be happy. You never really told us the whole story and I know that you don't like to talk about it but we all know that your parents hurt you. I'm sorry your mom left you. That had to be rough but that doesn't mean that every other female is going to leave you. Indie didn't leave you. You left her. Now you're both hurting and it's your fault. What are you going to do to fix it?"

I look up into Nico's kind eyes and swallow hard. *Is that what I've been doing?* All this time I thought that my dad had been the one to hurt me more because of the physical scars. I thought that I was pushing people away because I didn't want to let them have that much control over me. I didn't want them to ruin me like my mom had ruined my dad. *It wasn't love that ruined him. It was her leaving.*

The door bangs open and Nico and I both turn to see Atlas standing in the doorframe, looking pissed.

"See you later, Mischa," Nico says, squeezing past Atlas and heading back to his room.

Atlas kicks the door closed after him and I squeeze the chairs armrests. I hate when anyone is angry with me.

"What the hell are you doing?"

"Uh..." I look around the room, unsure what he's talking about.

"You're messing with my relationship and that's not okay. Darcy has been sleeping at Indie's place for the last five days. *FIVE DAYS*, Mischa."

I can't help it. I laugh out loud at that. The idea of not being able to go five days without someone just seems so dramatic to me. *You've been without Indie for ten and look how you're handling that.*

That thought sobers me and I nod at Atlas. "I'm sorry."

Atlas collapses onto my tattoo table. He looks tired. Almost as tired as me and I look down to my shoes.

"What are you doing, Mischa?" Atlas asks quietly and I swallow at the concern I can hear in his voice.

"What do you mean?"

"What are you doing with Indie? I know you two were sleeping together. Hell, the whole shop knows that. We also all know that you two aren't even talking now and both of you are unhappy."

I want to ask how Indie is. I want to pick up the phone and call her but what do I say?

"Mischa, Indie is a badass girl and she's fucking perfect for you. She's just as weird and bubbly and funny as you are. She's independent and she's not going to get clingy with you or anything. You're both loyal and smart and cool. Why aren't you together?"

"I don't do relationships. You know this," I say, defensively.

"You knew that Indie was falling for you. It was obvious. You know that she's the relationship type. So what, were you just messing with her this whole time?"

"NO!" I shout, appalled that he would even think that of me.

"Then what the hell have you been doing with her this whole time? If you knew that she was the relationship type, if you knew that she was falling in love with you. Why didn't you break it off sooner? Before someone got hurt."

Why didn't I? I knew that Indie was starting to like me a little too much. Why didn't I end it then? Why did I even break my rules and spend more than one night with her in the first place?

"Alright, my turn," Sam says as the door opens and she appears in the doorway.

Atlas stands turning to leave and I give him an apologetic look before I turn to face Sam.

"I think I've heard it all from everyone else," I say, trying to head her off.

"No, you haven't."

Her voice is determined and I can see her chin is lifted in that stubborn way of hers.

"Okay, hit me with it," I say with a sigh.

"I love you."

My mouth drops open and I stare at her. I love all of the guys at Eye Candy Ink, they're my family, but we've never said it to each other before.

"I love you, too," Atlas says, stepping back into the room.

"I love you," Nico says, appearing behind them.

"For the love of God," I mumble, feeling my cheeks heat

with a blush. I duck my head as Zeke pushes into my tiny room too.

"I love you, too," he says and then just because he's a dick he adds, "Son."

I flip him off and he steps past Sam, wrapping his arms around me in a hug.

"Oh my God," I wheeze as he crushes me.

Sam and Atlas immediately join him, hugging me. Atlas even rubs his cheek against mine and I can't help but laugh.

"Okay, stop"

"Nico get in here," Zeke calls and Nico lumbers over, wrapping his arms around all of us.

"This is my nightmare," I say but I can't stop the smile from practically splitting my face in two.

"Uh, hello?" A voice calls from up front and we all break apart, headed to greet the first client and get ready for the day.

I smile, twirling around in my chair but stop when I see Zeke is still standing in my doorway.

"You don't have to be afraid of love, Mischa. If Indie or some other girl breaks your heart, we'll be here to help piece you back together."

He nods down the hallway to the rest of the crew and I can feel my throat getting scratchy like I might cry.

"Thanks...dad."

"Anytime, son."

I crack a smile at that and he laughs, knocking twice on my doorframe before he heads down the hall toward his office. I spin around, grabbing my first tattoo from the stack of papers on my desk and head up front to greet my first client. I know that I'll have to figure all of this out with Indie but I need to get it straight in my head first.

12

I ndie

I MUST HAVE FALLEN asleep on the couch again. I groan, rolling onto my side as I rub my eyes and look around for what woke me up.

"Iiiinnnddiieee!" Someone sings outside my door, followed by someone tapping out an uneven beat against the wood.

"Mischa?" I ask, my voice coming out groggy.

It doesn't matter. He can't hear me over his drum solo. I pull myself off the couch, shuffling over to the door as I try to wake up. I have a feeling I'm going to need my wits about me to deal with him right now.

I unlock the door, swinging it open to reveal a very drunk Mischa leaning against the doorframe.

"Hey, boo."

"Boo?" I mumble as he pushes past me. "Mischa, are you drunk?"

I've never seen Mischa drink more than one or two beers. Now he's showing up here wasted?

"No, course not," he says, trying to look serious. He dissolves into laughter, crashing against the couch on his way to the hallway.

"What are you doing here? Where are you going?" I call after him, hurrying down the hallway to catch up with him.

He ignores me, heading into my room and straight for the bed. He pulls off his jacket, tossing it on the floor before he falls face first onto the mattress. I stand in shock as he buries his nose in my pillow and breathes deeply.

"Damn, Indie. I love the way you smell. Like cotton candy and unicorns or some shit."

"What do unicorns smell like?" I ask, unable to hide my smile.

"Like happiness... and maple syrup."

I laugh at that and walk over to the bed, sitting gingerly on the edge.

"What are you doing here, Mischa?" I ask again.

"I was just around the corner at Captain's," he says, his words only slightly slurring.

"Okay... and what are you doing *HERE*?" I try one last time.

He's silent for a while and I wonder if he passed out.

"I miss you," he mumbles into my pillow.

I don't know what to say to that so I just sit next to him, staring out the window at the dark river below.

"I think I'm fucked up, Indie," he says and his voice is so small.

"What?" I ask, doing my best to keep my voice steady. It feels like my heart breaks all over again at that statement.

"I started seeing a therapist. Today was my first appointment. It's Nico's parents. They're psychol-psychialogists," he slurs, scowling as he tries to come up with the right word.

"Psychologists?" I supply.

"That's the one," he says, tapping his nose and pointing at me as he tries to sit up next to me on the bed.

"He's just like them."

"Who?"

"Nico. He's just like his parents. They see everything, ya know what I mean?"

"Yeah," I say, wondering where all of this is going.

"He said something to me that just," he makes a blowing up motion with his hand next to his head.

"Nico's dad?"

"No, Nico," He rolls his eyes like I'm ridiculous for not being able to follow his story.

I wait for him to tell me what exactly Nico said that made his head explode but he just stares off into space.

"So, Nico said something and then you went out and got drunk?"

"I'm not drunk. I never get drunk. My dad used to get drunk all of the time and I never want to be like him. I don't get drunk. Just tipsy."

"Okay, but just so you're clear on this, being drunk doesn't mean being passed out."

He laughs out loud, the sound echoing back to us as it bounces off the walls and around my quiet room.

"You're so fucking funny, Indie." He eyes me for a moment, his eyes trailing over my face. "Why the fuck did you fall for me?" He asks quietly and I blink at him. "I'm not good enough for you. I'm a commitment-phobe with abandonment issues who hates being touched or feeling vulnerable."

He lists off all of his faults and I wonder just what exactly they talked about at therapy.

"I don't think that you can choose who you fall in love with, Mischa. I just did. I fell in love with you and that means loving the good parts and the messy parts. Everyone has sharp edges and smooth surfaces. I think that's what love is. Finding someone whose sharp edges don't cut you. You're a good guy. Loyal and honest and kind. That outweighs all of your hang ups for me. Your sharp edges don't bother me."

I shrug as he bites his bottom lip, mulling over my words.

"I like your sharp edges," he says with a playful smirk as he nods toward the window.

I grin, remembering the night he fucked me against the wall there. I want to say that maybe that means that he loves me too but that's something that he needs to figure out for himself. I promised myself that I would never beg for a man to love me and pointing that out feels dangerously close to doing that.

"So, therapy?" I ask, wanting us to get back to a safer topic.

He frowns, staring off into space again for a minute.

"Yeah. I think I needed to talk to someone. I haven't been sleeping well since we stopped," he trails off, waving a finger back and forth between us.

"Oh."

"I don't want to be alone, Indie. I don't want to be alone and you don't want to rely on anyone. What a pair we are."

I wrap my arms around my middle as he just blurts out my worst fear.

"I miss you, Indie. I wish I hadn't messed this up."

Me too, I think but I keep that to myself.

His fingers brush against my bare knee and I know that's my cue to cut this visit off.

"I need to get to bed," I say, standing and heading for the door.

"Okay," he says behind me and when I turn, I see him toeing off his shoes and laying back on the bed, his eyes falling closed as soon as his head hits the pillow.

"Uh, Mischa?" I ask but he's already out.

His soft snores fill the room and I wonder if I should try to wake him and make him leave. The dumb part of my heart beats faster, wanting to spend one more night next to him.

Just tonight. This can't become a thing, I chastise myself as I turn the bedroom light off and crawl onto the bed next to him. He rolls onto his side and throws an arm over me, his lips curling up slightly.

I don't want to fall asleep. If this is really going to be the last time that I cuddle next to this man, then I don't want to miss a minute of it. I must doze off at some point though and when I wake in the morning, Mischa is gone and there's only a scrap of paper on his pillow to prove that last night wasn't a dream.

I pick the paper up, squinting as I try to make out his messy writing. Two words stare back at me.

I'm sorry.

13

Mischa

I DON'T KNOW how I let Sam talk me into going out with her tonight but here I am, at Club Se7en, trying to avoid flirting girls while also not losing my hearing from the pounding bass line pouring out of the speakers next to me.

I take a sip from my beer bottle, keeping an eye on Sam at the bar. She's been over there for a while, waiting on drinks and trying to shake some Wall Street looking dude who keeps hitting on her. She looks bored out of her mind as the guy yells over the music, his hands moving in front of him. She ducks out of the way when he gets too close and almost hits her in the face, shooting him a dirty look that he doesn't even seem to notice as he drones on.

I smirk as the bartender finally sets her drinks down and she grabs them, spinning around and walking away without a second glance. The guy shoots a glare at her back and I can see him mumble *bitch* from here.

"This place is filled with douchebags," she declares as soon as she's made her way back to where I'm hiding.

"Then why did you want to come here?" I ask, my tone bored.

"Just thought you should get out. You've been so gloomy these last few weeks. It's all anyone can talk about," she says as she lifts her whiskey sour and downs half of it.

"Great," I mumble under my breath, taking another sip of my beer.

I had my second therapy appointment today. I shake my head, trying to clear away the painful memories that we dredged up during this session. *Maybe that explains why I'm out drinking again.*

My mind thinks back to what happened last week and my fingers tighten around my beer bottle. I can't do that again. I can't give Indie what she deserves, what she needs, so I need to leave her alone.

My heart aches and I rub my chest with my palm. *Why the fuck does that keep happening?* I eye the beer in my hand. *I'll start a healthier diet tomorrow*, I promise myself.

I look over at Sam and see she's scanning the crowd, her eyes flitting over the dark figures and squinting as she tries to make out some people standing in a different dark corner.

"Who are you looking for?" I ask and she jumps, her whiskey getting dangerously close to slipping over the edge of her glass.

"No one," she says but her voice comes out rushed, a sure sign that she's lying.

"Right," I drawl and she flips me off, trying to discreetly look around the room once more.

Club Se7en just opened a couple of weeks ago and is already the hottest spot in the city. Zeke's friend, Max, is actually part owner of the place which is how we were able to bypass the line and waltz right in.

"Hey, you two."

I turn and see Max emerging from a door next to us. He smiles as he walks our way, his eyes raking over Sam as she fidgets and shifts next to me. *Interesting*, I think as I smile and hold my hand out to shake his.

"Hey, man. Thanks for getting us in here," I say but he's not paying me any attention, his eyes locked on Sam.

"Hello, Samantha."

"It's Sam, Max*WELL,*" Sam snaps back.

I grin, leaning against the wall and sipping my beer as I watch the show.

"You look beautiful," Max says, stepping closer to her.

"Yeah, when Mischa said he wanted to take me out tonight, I decided to dress up for him," she says with a smirk, stepping into my side and wrapping her arm around my waist.

I choke on my sip of beer as Max shoots me a dirty look. Before I can correct him, a slinky blonde waitress comes up and taps his shoulder. She whispers in his ear for a minute, pointing to the bar and he nods.

"If you'll excuse me, I have to see to a problem."

He looks right at me when he says problem and I want to tell him that Sam is full of shit but she chooses that moment to lay her head against my shoulder. Max's glare intensifies and I'm positive that I'm two seconds away from getting his fist in my face when the blonde waitress tugs on his elbow.

"I'll find you later," he says to Sam.

"Don't bother. I'll be occupied."

A muscle in Max's jaw ticks as he turns and stalks away. *I've got to get out of here before he comes back here and murders me.*

"Listen, Sam. I'm flattered, really, but I just don't see you like-"

"Oh, shut up!" She says, punching me in the arm. "I just needed him to think I was taken so that he stops bothering me. I'm for sure not into you like that and everyone knows that you love Indie," Sam says, rolling her eyes.

"I'm not in love with Indie!" I growl, my voice coming out louder than I had intended. "I don't do love. Anyone who says that they're in love is a dumb sucker who needs to see a physician about all of these delusions they're having. I am not, and will never, love someone."

A distressed sound comes from behind me and I spin around to see a pale, wide eyed Indie looking like she was just slapped.

"Indie, I-" but she turns and disappears back into the crowd.

"Way to go, asshole."

My stomach sinks and the ache in my chest grows as I watch her go. *Maybe I'm having a heart attack.* I know that I only reacted that strongly because of everything that we talked about in therapy today but that was still a dick move.

I'm not even sure that I actually still believe it.

Here I am, in a club with scantily clad woman, half of which have been eye fucking me since I walked in and I feel nothing. I don't want any of them. All because I would rather spend time with Indie then a string of random girls.

For the millionth time, I think back to what she said love was.

"I don't think that you can choose who you fall in love with, Mischa. I just did. I fell in love with you and that means loving

the good parts and the messy parts. Everyone has sharp edges and smooth surfaces. I think that's what love is. Finding someone whose sharp edges don't cut you. You're a good guy. Loyal and honest and kind. That outweighs all of your hang ups for me. Your sharp edges don't bother me."

No one can seem to tell me a definitive answer to that question, but out of all of the answers I've gotten, I like Indie's the best. I don't want something like what Atlas and Darcy have, where they can't bear to be apart for longer than thirty seconds. I like what Indie and I had. We had space. We went to work and then, because Indie is a workaholic, she came home and worked some more, but after that, we could hang out. Eat, watch tv, tell each other dumb jokes, just relax. I didn't need to be on her mind nonstop. We never texted each other good morning or good night like Atlas and Darcy do, but we would send each other memes once or twice a day, laughing and arguing over whose was funnier. Just little things to let each other know that we were thinking about them.

Fuck, was I in a relationship with Indie this whole time?

That question keeps rolling around in my head as I walk Sam out to her car and make sure she gets in okay. She shoots me a worried look as I close her door and head to my own car. It's been a rough day and I just want to be alone. I need to figure out what the hell to do about this mess I've made.

14

I ndie

"WE NEED MORE of those bite size bacon donuts," I inform Darcy and Atlas, standing on my tiptoes to try to see over the crowd to where the food truck is.

"How are you still eating?" Darcy asks, groaning as she rubs her hand over her stomach.

I've already made us try one of each thing from the food stands here at the carnival. Deep fried Oreos, bite size donuts, loaded French fries, and all of the other usual carnival food. I've been pigging out, comfort eating, after that mess with Mischa the other night.

I haven't talked to him since. He's tried to call and text me but I'm just not ready to hear from him. I can't deal with any more of his wishy-washy attitude. He needs to make a decision. Either he wants to be with me, or he doesn't.

I met Darcy and Atlas at the carnival in town after work.

It's late but the weather held and it's a balmy 82 degrees. I had changed out of my skinny jeans and into a short purple skirt and a thin tank top camisole with unicorns all over it. Darcy is dressed similarly in a pair of cutoff jean shorts and a tank top. I smiled when I first saw her. It wasn't that long ago that she was trying to hide her body in baggy clothes, too self-conscious of her curves. Atlas and his love of all of her have really helped her to see just how awesome and beautiful she is.

Most of the kids and families had left for the day by the time we got here. The bright game stands and flashing light bulbs on the rides help illuminate the streets as we navigate past teenagers running wild. We walk past the Tilt-A-Whirl and the music is so loud that I have to lean in close and yell to Darcy over it.

"What ride do you guys want to go on next?" I ask when I see Atlas lean down and nuzzle Darcy's neck.

They're so stinkin cute together but it's awkward enough being the third wheel without them getting all lovey-dovey on me.

"Um, how about..." Darcy drifts off as she looks around at the choices.

"Hey, isn't that Mischa?" Atlas asks, pointing behind me.

My back stiffens and I straighten my shoulders before I slowly turn around to look at where he's pointing. Sure enough, Mischa is winding his way through the crowd, heading in our direction. I spin around, narrowing my eyes at Atlas. He's been on his phone an awful lot this evening. He meets my eyes, a light blush staining his cheeks and making him look guilty as hell.

"Hey, guys," Mischa says from behind me and I send one last glare at Atlas before I turn to face him.

"Hi."

"Well, we'll let you two talk," Atlas says, shooting Mischa a look before he grabs Darcy's hand and drags her away.

"You arranged this, didn't you?"

"Yeah. You wouldn't answer my calls or texts and I needed to talk to you."

"Maybe I didn't want to talk to you. Did you ever think about that?"

"Indie, just let me-"

"No! You listen, Mischa. I'm not doing this anymore. You need to decide. Do you like me? Do you want more with me? I can't do anymore of this one step forward, two steps back with you."

He swallows hard, looking around wildly and I can't take it anymore. I huff, throwing my arms up and spinning on my heel.

"Wait!"

I keep walking.

"Wait, wait," he says as his hand grabs my arm. "Okay, Indie. Yeah, I like you. I miss you. Can we talk? Please? I just want things to go back to the way they were. Can we do that? Can we just go back to before?" He pleads, his fingers tightening around my bicep.

"No, I'm sorry Mischa, but we stopped because I wanted more. I don't want to go back to the way things were. I want something new, something more with you."

"I can't do more, Indie! You know that."

"Can't? Or won't?"

His chest rises and falls rapidly as his eyes search my face, looking for reason.

"I want more. I *deserve* more, a real relationship. I'm sorry you don't feel the same. I... I think we should stop seeing each other for a little while."

I can feel my eyes starting to well with tears and I jerk

my arm away, spinning around and heading toward the first ride that I see. I can feel his eyes boring into my back as I blindly hand my tickets over to the bored ride operator guy, climbing onto the Ferris wheel cart. It sways with my weight and I brush away a loose tear, turning to look around when the cart sways again, signaling that someone else climbed on after me.

Mischa sits across from me, eyeing me warily as the ride operator closes the door and the wheel starts to turn. His fingers grip the seat, his knuckles turning white as he holds the edge in a death grip.

"I don't want to stop seeing you."

"And I don't want to be friends with benefits anymore."

"Damnit, Indie. I don't do love. You know that!" He looks away, his face going pale as we start to get higher.

"What's wrong with you?" I ask, studying his stiff posture and how fidgety he's acting.

"I don't like heights," he mumbles, staring down at his feet.

"You don't like heights? Why the hell did you follow me onto a ferris wheel then?"

"I needed to talk to you," He pauses, looking up when the Ferris wheel comes to a stop.

"We did talk. Nothing has changed, Mischa."

"You were upset. You know I can't stand it when you're sad. I just wanted to make sure you were okay and- Jesus Christ! Why the fuck aren't we moving?" He screams over the edge.

"Other people are getting on," I say, trying to bite back my smile.

"Fucking death trap. The things I do for this crazy ass girl. I swear to God, I'm-"

"You know I can hear you right?"

He shoots a glare my way and I grin back at him, rocking gently.

"Stop that," He orders.

"What did you want to talk to me about?"

"Stop fucking rocking. I'm not dying on this thing today."

"Just spit it out, Mischa."

"I want... I want to try, okay?" He glares at me as he says the words, making the whole thing just a little less romantic than what I had pictured. His icy glare doesn't stop my heart from beating out of control in my chest though.

"Why? You don't do relationships. You don't do love. It's "for suckers", remember?" I say, using air quotes.

"Well, then I'm a fucking sucker."

The wheel starts to move and we do one full lap as I wait for Mischa to say the words I've been desperate to hear for weeks. We get to the top, our eyes locked on each other instead of the view, when there's a clunking sound and suddenly the wheel comes to a screeching halt.

Mischa's eyes widen to comical size and I peek over the side. The operator is messing around with the controls and I sit back, resting against the hard-plastic seat as I wait for Mischa to start talking or the world to start spinning again. I swear it came to a stop when he said that he was a sucker and it hasn't stopped moving again since.

"Mischa."

He looks at me, his eyes panicked as he tries to sit perfectly still and not look down.

"It's okay," I say, slowly sliding around to his side of the cart.

I reach him and climb into his lap, straddling him.

"It's okay. I've got you."

He stares into my eyes, his fingers digging into my hips as he swallows hard.

"I'm a sucker, Indie. Fuck, I know that I'm a bad bet. I know that I'll mess up and I probably don't deserve you but, I fell for you. Jesus, I don't even know when it happened, but it did."

"Say the actual words, Mischa."

He gulps, his eyes wide and trusting like a child's as he watches me.

"I love you, Indie."

"About time," I say a second before I crush my lips to his.

15

M ischa

"JESUS, INDIE, RIGHT NOW?"

"Uh huh," she moans in my ear, wiggling on my lap. "Don't you want me?"

"I always fucking want you, but I really, really hate heights. I don't even think I could get hard right now. Not while we're rocking around way up here," I say, squeezing my eyes shut when I accidentally look over the edge of the car.

"I think you can," Indie whispers in my ear. "You could fuck me in this ferris wheel cart right now, in front of all of these people and no one would even know."

Fuck. My cock hardens into steel inside my jeans and I shift as Indie keeps whispering in my ear. I should have known she'd be able to override my fear of heights. I swear,

her voice has a direct line to my cock. One word, one sylla-
ble, from her delectable little mouth and I'm ready to go.

"You could take me bare right now. I'd walk around the
rest of this carnival with you dripping out of me."

"Jesus," I moan as I frantically rip at my belt and the
button on my jeans.

Indie giggles, shifting on top of me to help me out.
Thank god she wore a skirt today. She goes to stand, to pull
her panties down, I guess, but I can't wait. I reach between
us, sliding the thin lace to the side before I thrust up into
her slick heat. We both groan when I'm fully seated inside
her and I reach up, pulling the edge of her thin tank top
down until her small tits are exposed. I wrap my lips around
one sensitive bud as she starts to move on top of me. *Fuck,
I've missed this, missed her.* I look up, locking eyes with Indie
and she smiles like she can feel it too, this rightness, as she
starts to slowly ride me.

"I love you, Indie."

"I know. I love you too."

Her lips meet mine and we move together slowly, our
bodies rocking together as we slowly slip down off the ferris
wheel seat. Once I'm sitting on the floor, our rhythm picks
up and soon she's riding me hard. Her face is tipped up
toward the sky and she's lost in her pleasure and it's the best
thing that I've ever seen.

Indie has always been my sun, my bright light leading
me out of the darkness. I don't know if I just didn't see it
earlier or if I just didn't want to admit it to myself but it's
true. She blew into my life and illuminated everything that I
was missing. She had me breaking every single one of my
stupid rules and it was the best thing that I ever did.

I can feel the familiar tingle in my balls as Indie tightens
around me, her breath coming out in short pants. Her

thighs flex next to me and my fingers tighten on her hips as I help her move over me.

"Fuck, you're so wet," I groan as I feel Indie start to reach her peak. "Is it the public sex or me saying that I love you?" I whisper in her ear and she goes off like a bomb.

She calls my name but it gets lost in the wind and the music blaring from some other nearby ride. She clamps down on my length, squeezing like a vice and I groan, my fingers tightening so much that I know I'm leaving bruises but she doesn't seem to mind.

My head falls back against the hard plastic seat and I smile up as the bright lights warm my face. The ride chooses that moment to start up again and Indie and I scramble to right our clothes as the operator stops at each car to let people off. She scampers off of my lap, standing up as I tuck myself back into my jeans. She pulls her tank top up, covering her tits back up but her nipples are still stiff peaks, poking against the fabric of her shirt like they want my mouth wrapped around them again. Her skirt falls down but not before I see some of my cum already leaking out of her.

I get hard all over again but it's finally our turn and I offer Indie my hand, helping her off. She tries to pull away once we're back on solid ground but I stop her, intertwining our fingers as we walk off in search of our friends.

I know that I have a long way to go before I'm completely comfortable with all of this relationship stuff but I want to try. Indie is worth it to me. I know that she'll be there for me every step of the way and my life will never be boring with her in it. She makes me laugh more than anyone I've ever met. She pushes me outside my comfort zone, pushes me to be a better person, to be a better friend.

She's my sun, the other half to my soul, and I love her.

16

I ndie

I BRACE my elbows on the counter, watching as Mischa stirs something in a big pot on the stove. It's his day off and we've been having a lazy day, lying around in our pajamas watching TV. I think we're both still tired from helping Atlas and Darcy move into their apartment downstairs earlier this week. *Who knew they had that much stuff?* Mischa ran to the store an hour ago and came back to make dinner while I checked my emails and worked for a little bit, but now that that's done, I can finally broach the subject that's been on my mind all week.

"So..."

"What?" Mischa asks, glancing over his shoulder at me.

"We've been spending a lot of time over here."

"Yeah, I live here. Where did you want to spend time?"

"Here is fine," I say, grinning at him. He looks at me like I'm crazy and I smile wider.

"What if I lived here too?"

He drops the spoon and it clunks against the side of the pot. I roll my eyes. *He's so dramatic.*

"Why would you want to live here too?"

"Cause Darcy is right downstairs."

He starts stirring the pot again.

"Oh, and you're here and all of my stuff is already here."

"What?" He asks, his brow scrunched in confusion as he glances around the kitchen and living room.

I don't know how he didn't notice all of my stuff showing up here. I guess because he's really only here to crash and I've been sleeping here for the last two weeks so it makes sense that *some* of my stuff would be here, but a waffle maker and some throw pillows? I roll my eyes at his lack of observation.

Mischa is still looking around the room and I give him a minute. My boyfriend has come a long way but he still tends to freak if you bring up relationship stuff. I've learned if you give him a second to adjust that he's usually okay.

He still goes to therapy once a week and it's really helped. They've already made so much progress. He can even say "I love you" now without wincing. So much progress!

"Alright. Let's do it."

"We're doing this *thang*?" I ask excitedly and his shoulders shake with his laughter.

"Yeah, we're doing this *thang*," he says, finally setting the spoon down and coming around the counter to wrap me up in his arms.

"I love you, Indie."

"Love you more, Mischy."

"Don't call me Mischy."

"But we need cute pet names for each other!"

"No, we really don't."

I smile as he goes back to the stove. *I'll wear him down.* I drag my computer closer to me, bringing up the email I had been writing. I smile as I hit send on the message to my landlord, letting him know that I wouldn't be renewing my lease.

I know this might not seem like a big step but for Mischa and I, it's huge. It might be years before he's ready to get married or have kids or any of that, and a lot of girls might get annoyed or impatient of waiting, but I know that Mischa loves me. I know that he gets up every day and tries for me. It's been a learning curve for him to go from so anti-relation-ship to being in one. I know I'll have to teach him about anniversaries and all of that, but for right now, for this one moment, everything is perfect.

17

M ischa

I FEEL like I'm going to throw up.

Is that normal in this situation? My hands are clammy and I have an irrational fear that I'm going to drop the ring and it's going to get lost and then what? My fingers tighten around it until the diamond digs into my palm and I take a deep breath. Indie will be home any minute and I don't want her to walk in and see me looking like I'm about to pass out.

The doorknob turns and there she is. My light. The best fucking thing that ever happened to me. I clear my throat and she looks up from the mail that she's shuffling in her hands.

"Hey, Mischy! How was your day?"

Outwardly, I roll my eyes at the nickname just like I have every day for the last two years but inside I'm smiling.

"It was alright. How about you?"

"Long, but productive," she says as she finally tosses the mail on the counter and kicks off her shoes. "Did you want to go downstairs and see Darcy and Atlas with me?" She asks and her eyes light up when she thinks about Darcy. Those two are still super close and most days I have to go down there and drag her out of their apartment.

My heart starts to race as I think about Indie and I being married like them, but not in fear. I'm not afraid of relationships or the future anymore.

"Yeah, but first, I wanted to show you something."

I lead her over to the kitchen where, on the counter, is the list that I wrote when I was a dumb kid. The one that was supposed to keep me safe and protected. I watch as Indie's eyes scan down it and she frowns as she reads over the list.

Stay Safe Rules:

1. No dates.
2. No buying a girl dinner. Or breakfast.
3. No spending the night.
4. No sleeping with a girl for more than one night.
5. Never get involved with someone you know.
6. No touching outside of sex.
7. No meaningful conversations with girls.
8. No public displays of affection.
9. No girl roommates.
10. No mention of the L word.

"WHAT IS THIS?" She asks, her amethyst eyes meeting mine.

"Those were my rules. As long as I followed them, I'd never fall in love and I was supposed to be safe... but I broke those first two when I bought you some soft pretzels and we walked around downtown."

She looks back to the list and I go on.

"I broke the third one the first night that we slept together."

Her smile grows and in turn, so does mine.

"Rules four and five, rule six," I say as I take her hand in mine, bringing it to my lips and kissing the back. Tears shimmer in her eyes and I rush to finish. I hate seeing her cry, even happy tears.

"Rule seven I broke the night I told you about my scars. Rule eight I broke on that Ferris wheel, we regularly break Rule ten, and rule nine I broke when you moved in here with me."

"You think I'm your *roommate*?" She asks in mock outrage and I grin at her.

"Well, you do pay half the rent."

She throws her head back and laughs at that.

"Why are you showing me this?"

"Because there's one last rule. Flip it over."

As soon as she reaches for the paper, I drop down on one knee and pull the diamond ring from my pocket. She spins around, her eyes filling with tears as I hold the ring out to her.

"Indie Hearst, I love you. You're the only girl that I've ever loved and that I ever will love. What do you say? Do you wanna do this *thang* with me?"

I hold my breath, my heart racing in my chest as I wait for her to answer me.

"Oh gosh, you sound so romantic right now," she says with a laugh as a few tears spill over and slip down her cheeks.

"Yeah, 90's slang always makes people sound romantic," I say dryly, still down on one knee.

"Say it again."

"Indie, marry me. Let's do this thang."

"Yes!"

She tackles me back onto the carpet, her arms locked around my neck and her black hair falling in my face. I grin into her neck, crushing her to me.

"Oh my GOD! I need to go tell Darcy!"

She pushes off me and is halfway out the door before she realizes that I'm still laying on the ground with the ring.

"That's mine," she says, plucking the ring from my hand. "Come on!"

I push to my feet and laugh as I trail after her, but not before I grab the champagne from the fridge and the note from the counter. I glance down, smiling at the eleventh and final rule.

Meet Indie Hearst and say fuck it all.

18

I ndie

THREE YEARS LATER...

I TUG on Mischa's hand, trying to coax him to move faster but he pulls me back.

"For the love of God, Indie. You're going to slip and fall and drag me down and then what?" He asks, his free hand going to my stomach as he cradles my baby bump.

We found out I was pregnant at the same time as Darcy and Atlas. As in, Darcy and I took pregnancy tests together one night and Mischa and Atlas had come home to find us crying and hugging each other. They freaked out, thinking something bad had happened and we were so excited that we could barely tell them. Eventually we did though and they had each taken it in their own way.

Atlas had hugged Darcy, beaming at her. Mischa had grabbed me and told me to stop jumping up and down. He's read approximately one hundred baby books already and he probably knows more about babies at this point than I do. He's adorable though, waking up each Monday and telling me how big our baby has grown and what new developments are happening.

We found out that we're having a baby boy like Darcy and Atlas are and I know that Atlas and Mischa are hoping that they're best friends too. Everyone at the shop is excited for us. I'm not supposed to know, but they're throwing Darcy and I a joint baby shower next week.

I know that Mischa is over preparing and that he's nervous to be a dad, scared that he'll mess up somehow. He's already talking about us getting a bigger place and about childcare. Luckily, my office is letting me work from home and we already started looking for nannies to watch Darcy and Atlas's baby and ours over at our place.

We've got this being pregnant thing down pat. Now, if only Mischa could move just a little bit faster. There's a new ice cream place opening up down the street that's selling rolled ice cream. I've been craving sweets ever since I got pregnant with the little one and Mischa promised me ice cream after our final ultrasound appointment but it's almost lunch time and if he doesn't hurry, there's going to be a long line.

"Indie," he says, tugging on my hand and spinning me around to face him. "Listen, I promise that I will get you and our little man some ice cream, but you have to slow down. You're going to give me a heart attack."

I sigh but walk at a more reasonable pace. I can hear him muttering to himself about crazy women but I just grin.

"Love you, Mischy."

"I love you more, Indie," he says, tugging me closer into his side and kissing the top of my head before he opens the door to the ice cream parlor for me.

"Now, what flavor do you want?"

"Um, a cookies and cream one, the cheesecake one, and the fudge brownie one," I tell him, practically drooling as I think about all of it.

"I can feed you lunch too," he says.

"This is lunch."

"Like a real lun-, ya know what. Three ice creams, coming up," he says, kissing me quick on the lips before he goes to wait in line. I grab a booth in the back and watch him.

Mischa went from being a commitment phobe with a list of rules a mile long to the best husband and soon to be father that I could ever ask for. He doesn't give a shit how much money I make or if I want to paint our bathroom pink or if I order three ice creams for lunch. He's the perfect guy, at least for me.

Who would have thought at the start of all of this that I would ever actually get my happily ever after?

Mischa looks over at me, his blue eyes softening as he smiles at me. I know that everything is going to be alright. I caught my unicorn and we're surrounded by great friends and the family that we want, that we chose. Our baby boy kicks then, and I know that he is agreeing with me.

Or I thought he was. My water chooses that moment to break and I gasp as I feel it trickle down my leg. Before I know it, I'm calling for Mischa. I've never seen him move so fast in my life. He wraps his arm around my back, helping me out of the booth and hustling me outside. He's already calling Atlas and asking him to meet us at the hospital as we hurry over a block to his car.

He buckles me in and his eyes look a little wild.

"You know, I never got my ice cream."

He freezes at that, his hands resting on my stomach as he huffs out a laugh.

"Jesus, I love you, Indie."

"I love you, too. Now let's go to the hospital and have this kid already!"

"Yeah, let's do this thang."

STAY TUNED!

*Sam's story is coming soon!

ABOUT THE AUTHOR

CONNECT WITH ME!

If you enjoyed this story, please consider leaving a review on Amazon or any other reader site or blog that you like. Don't forget to recommend it to your other reader friends.

If you want to chat with me, please consider joining my VIP list or connecting with me on one of my Social Media platforms. I love talking with each of my readers. Links below!

❥ VIP list
❥ shawhartbooks.com

ALSO BY SHAW HART